THE MIMOSA TREE

Also by Vera and Bill Cleaver

GROVER

WHERE THE LILIES BLOOM

LADY ELLEN GRAE

ELLEN GRAE

THE
MIMOSA
TREE

⋙⋘

Vera & Bill
CLEAVER

⋙⋘

J. B. Lippincott Company

PHILADELPHIA NEW YORK

THE MIMOSA TREE

CHAPTER ONE

The last of the Proffitts' hogs lay dying in the afternoon sun. It lay on its side in the black mud within the sty trying to draw air into its poisoned lungs. It struggled for each breath and when the last one came it rolled over, squealed once, flickered its dim, white eyes, and was finally still.

Leaning against the rough railing surrounding the sty, Marvella Proffitt traced an aimless pattern in the brown earth with a bare foot. Tall and awkward for her fourteen years, she felt again the strife of communication that had always been between herself and her father. Vaguely it angered her, this inability. Since Zollie had come it had grown worse. Big and faded-blonde and blowzy, Zollie was never short on words. From morning to night her talk of things she had done and things she intended to do filled the Proffitts' tar-papered house, flowed from its doors and windows in a loud, bright, confident stream. She was never still and the little kids loved her vulgar laughter and her brittle chatter. They trailed after her like puppies.

It was Zollie's idea that the Proffitts pull up their stakes in Goose Elk and migrate to Chicago. Maybe they'd go tomorrow now that the hog, which had been their last tie, was dead. Marvella pushed a handful of tangled red hair back from her face and spoke to her father. "Well, that's the last of them."

"The Critchers done it," said her father. "Can't nobody tell me they didn't. Can't you nor Zollie nor the law nor anybody else tell me they didn't. It's their kind of work."

"Pa," said Marvella. "It don't differ now. Don't you see that? Nothing differs now except for us to get ourselves out of here as fast as we can. Zollie's ready and so am I and so are the little kids. All we're doing is waiting for you to say when you are."

Dorman Proffitt raised his sightless eyes to the pleasant hills surrounding his twenty-two acres. A buffet of heated air swept over him. Already he smelled the stench from the dead hog and the blight from the fields—of potatoes rotting in the ground and other truck rotting on stems and vines—reached him in a helpless, desperate wave. "I don't see how we can do it," he said. "It smells bad now and I know it must look thataway but it's all we've ever had that was all ours. Your mama and me started here the day we was married and we worked like mules tryin' to put it together and keep it that way. I jest don't see how we can leave it."

Somberly Marvella looked beyond her father's shaggy head to the silent hills. The yellow light over them was clear and bright. The trees on their green slopes were motionless. She compressed her lips. "We just do it, that's all. The car's packed. All we're waiting for is for you to say when. The hog's dead now. We should go tomorrow."

Beneath the frosty fringe of his hair Dorman Proffitt's milky eyes yearned. "If only your mama was alive to say was we doin' the right thing. Zollie's good. I know she means good. A man couldn't ask for a better wife or better mother to his young-uns. But it ain't the same. I hear her say we got to go and I know more'n likely it's the truth but it jest don't sink in." With his clenched fist he beat on the sty railing.

Flies had been attracted to the dead hog. Tumbling and buzzing they began to settle down onto the body of it. Marvella turned her head and cautiously looked into the face of her father. It was too old for its actual age. The mountain air which, according to flatlanders, toned and glowed complexions, hadn't done a thing favorable for his. Leathered by wind and sun it was brown and permanently creased. Only the blurred eyes with the milky veil over them remained curiously young. The eyes lent an innocent look to his face.

He's the father of me and all the four little kids, thought Marvella, and still he doesn't see what's best for us. Why is that?

Her father was still beating on the sty railing with his fist but had forgotten that he was doing it. She went away from him and around the corner of the house and over to the car which had been backed to the front steps. The weight of what had already been stored in it had taken an early toll. The rear tires had flattened perceptibly and the long, cream-colored hood, spotted with rust, had risen to a new stature. She sat on one of its fenders and looked out across the fields to the bright hills but did not see them. Chicago, she thought, and something in her brain swam fluidly and her heart, knocked in small, velvety strokes.

Zollie was not afraid of the cream-colored car, though by her own admission she had never driven anything mechanical until her marriage to Dorman Proffitt. Majestically she sat behind the wheel of it and steered them down the narrow, winding mountain road to the main highway that would take them to Chicago. Hunched small and still beside her, Dorman Proffitt sat with a set face and clenched fists. In the back seat Marvella sat flanked by the four little kids. They were glad to be going away from the mountains to the city. Concentrating on the excitement of what was happening to them they said, "Tell again where we're agoing to live, Marvella."

She smiled with them. "In a tall, white house where other families live. There'll be BIG stores nearby."

Arlie, four and fair and sturdy, slid a pink thumb into his mouth. "Where you can buy anything you want. All kinds of candy."

"Yes. All kinds."

"It won't be like at Goose Elk," Dwain said. "In Chicago there are lights at night and lots of people. How many people, Marvella?"

"I don't know. Millions, Zollie said."

Dwain's eyes, bright blue in his freckled face, shone with pleasure. "We'll be friends with them, won't we?"

"Sure."

"They won't always awanting to be fighting with us like them old Critchers down in the holler, will they?"

"Oh, no. City people don't fight with each other. They don't like to fight."

Without any silliness in his statement Noah said, "They're rich and we'll be rich, too. Zollie says so. She says we're going to have a toilet right inside the house and a television box and each have our own bed. We aren't going to grow any more potatoes or cabbage or hogs. We'll buy what we eat at the big stores. Zollie's going to be a maid in the BIG hotel where her sister works and is going to make lots of money for us. When we're bigger we'll work, too. All of us. And make so much money we won't know what to do with it all. Zollie says so."

Hugh, the belligerent one, was being obedient and interested. "Marvella won't have to wait to get any bigger," he said. "She's big enough now. Aren't you, Marvella?"

"Yes," she answered and, thinking of her future self, hugged them and urged them to have a final look at the mountains they would never see again and laughed when they said they didn't care, for she didn't either. Her father had his head out the window now and she thought he might be crying but Zollie wasn't paying him any heed. Driving them to their new and better life she was singing and the trees were rushing past, their trunks shining silver in the honey-colored morning. In the distance the heath and grass and sedge balds of the Great Smokies were stark against the blue sky bowl. In the low bushes along the roadside small animals scuttled and out of a mass of rhododendron and laurel, all twisted together, a band of chimney swifts, sooty black, crackled up and out.

After three days of traveling, eating their food cold from cans, sleeping in the car in areas designated for rest, and washing themselves in filling-station rest rooms, they reached Chicago and the house of Zollie's sister. Her name was Juanita and she acted glad to see them. She fed them a hot, hurry-meal of slumgullion and light bread spread with oleo and then herded them up the bare, shadowed stairway to the apartment over her own. She unlocked its door and flung it wide and said, "Your new home," and they went in and looked at the four rooms, all of them with pink-painted walls. Juanita described its kitchen as "efficient." She showed them how the pink stove worked and displayed the ice cubes freezing in the pink refrigerator. The little kids discovered the bathroom and right away each had to try the toilet. A television set on four legs stood in one corner of the front room. Juanita went to it and pulled a knob and almost immediately there was motion on its screen—a beautiful girl on a hospital bed, crying and writhing.

Zollie and Juanita returned to the kitchen to talk in lowered voices about the advantages of the apartment and the price. The owner didn't care so much about the money, Juanita said. He was more interested in good, reliable, conscientious tenants. The money came second. She said they could pay by the week at first if they wanted. Zollie said that would be a help and reached into the bodice of her dress, withdrew the Proffitt savings and counted out several bills.

The little kids were still in the bathroom flushing the toilet. Arlie was shouting that it was his turn and Hugh was telling him to shut up. The others were laughing. "You got to push the handle all the way down, like this, see? And then the water goes out of it and then it fills up again."

In the kitchen Zollie and Juanita were talking now in normal tones. About Juanita's job at the hotel, how much she made in salary and how much in tips. About how nice some people were who lived there, how stinking mean others. The manager was expecting Zollie. He wasn't always fair with the maids but there were ways to get even with him. Zollie should take it easy at first though. Juanita had every Thursday off. She'd arrange it so that Zollie could have the same. They lowered their voices and whispered.

The girl on the television screen had stopped crying. A nurse had come to soothe her, was helping her sit up, was holding a glass of water to her lips. She didn't look a bit sick, except for her eyelids which were shiny black. The girl's nakedness, shining through the white stuff of her gown, embarrassed Marvella. She glanced at her father who had uncertainly sat down on a chair near the window. She said, "This is a nice place, Pa. We can be comfortable here."

Her father turned his face toward the television set. "What is that thing? A radio?"

"It's a television set, Pa."

"Like the one in Hawkins' store?"

"No, this one's bigger."

"Tell me," said her father, "what's outside the window. Look and tell me what's out there."

She went to the window and looked through the net curtains and saw a gray, grim wall, only four or five feet removed from her. She looked down into the alley between the buildings and saw the refuse littered there: overflowing garbage cans, an old stained mattress with the stuffing spilled, a wicker chair without a seat. Broken glass glinted in the gutters. Down in the far end of the alley a pile of blackened rags smoldered. An old man shuffled out from a doorway and leaned in it, then went over and stirred the rags with his foot and sparks erupted. He went back to his doorway and leaned against it again, staring out at the decay. Zollie had parked the Proffitts' car up close to the buildings. It had two missing hub caps. Its hood and the top of it were begrimed.

Among all this two dark-skinned children were playing catch-ball. There weren't any trees or flowers. She looked up expecting to see the sky. The sky wasn't there. There were only the heads of tall buildings, cramped close together. Above these, where the sky should have been, there was a layer of thick, oily smoke. Dark and unmoving, it seemed pasted there. She waited for it to dissipate as smoke should, but it didn't move. She turned back to her father.

"Wal?" he said. "What's out there?"

His old-young face with the eyes straining and the mouth folded flat was too anxious. He wants there to be trees and flowers and birds out there, she thought. Like at home. It'll kill him if I say there's just trash and mess. It'd just about kill him. He'd want to go back home and we can't do that. The car wouldn't make it and besides there's nothing to go back for. He's a country man—all of us are country people— but the country drove us out. Now we're in the city where we can make money and not have to worry about the Critchers poisoning our hogs and the blight killing our crops and the snow coming six feet deep in the wintertime. This is a nice place. All the pink makes me a little sick to my stomach but I'll get used to it. The little kids have got their inside toilet and there's the television and tomorrow I'm going to get me a job. I can be a maid. Maybe not in Juanita's hotel but I can get to be one if I try. All you have to do is say, "Yes, ma'am," and "No, ma'am," and know how to clean. I'm smart. I learn fast. Everybody says so. And I'm not afraid of things. Even Zollie has to say that about me. So we've got to stay here for a while. Until we can see our way clearer than we can now. So I've got to say to him there are trees and birds and flowers out there.

She said, "Pa."

He leaned forward. "Wal? Wal, what's out there?"

"Trees," she answered. "And birds and flowers. Not as many as at home but enough. It's all behind a big, white fence so you can't get in to touch any of it though. In a city like this, Pa, they got to have fences. There're so many people and cars and all."

"Yes, yes," said her father. "I c'n understand that. I jest wanted to know, that's all. What was out there. How it looked. Is the trees green?"

"Yes, Pa."

"What kind are they?"

She squinted and then, concentrating, squinted harder. An imaginary row of trees sprung into view. One of them, bigger than the rest, stood out clearly. It looked old and very strong. It appeared to her the most noble thing she had ever seen. Beneath it clumps of bluets flourished and at its back and over its head wet clouds streamed.

"Marvella?"

"Yes, Pa?"

"I asked you what kind was the trees. Can you tell?"

"Mostly they're firs, Pa. Except one. There's one mimosa tree. It's huge, the biggest one I ever saw."

"And the flowers. What color's they?"

"White. Some pink. There are a lot of blue ones."

Her father released his sigh. He eased his feet from his shoes. The anxiety was going from him. "Wal," he said. " 'Twas a long trip and I'm tired. Fetch me something to prop my feet up on, Marvella. Maybe I'll jest take me a little nap."

The layer of oily smoke over the columns of the buildings was still there. She went away from the window and searched in one of the other rooms for a stool and found one. The little kids would have to be told about the flowers and trees growing in the alley. She'd have to create the picture for them, make them see how important it was. They wouldn't snitch on her; they never did. Neither would Zollie. Zollie might laugh but she wouldn't snitch. Zollie understood things when she wanted to.

꧁꧂

CHAPTER TWO

꧁꧂

The dark-skinned children who played catch-ball in the alley, leaving the game sometimes to go and rake through the garbage for trophies, were suspicious of the Proffitts. "Where youse from?" they demanded.

Hugh, the belligerent, walked up to them. "Why you want to know?"

They grinned and hooked their thumbs in their belts. "You hillbilly, ain't you?"

"No."

"You are so."

"We are not. We're from North Carolina."

They shrieked with laughter. "That's hillbilly! That's *real* hillbilly! Whatsa matter you? You not even know your own self what you are?"

Strangely, Hugh turned humbly patient with them. "We're from Goose Elk, North Carolina. That's in the hills all right but it's *different*."

"Goose Elk!" they screamed and ran around gathering up

tomato cans and throwing them into the air. They were skinny and dirty and smelled strongly of garlic. Both had long black hair which curled stiffly around their ears. Obsessed with their glee they fell upon the old stained mattress and rolled about. They stood up and capered back. "This is our alley."

Hugh flushed. His eyes were grave and steady. "I reckon we can see that but we won't hurt it. We just want to play in it."

Their black unwinking eyes considered. "You find anything valuable in it it belongs to us. That has got to be understood."

"Anything valuable we find belongs to you," said Hugh. "All right. We understand that."

"What valuable?" asked Noah. "Nothing out here except trash. What could we find valuable?"

Now the dark-skinned boys were very serious. "Sometimes," they said, "people throw things out by mistake and we find them. Only last week we found a picture frame. Solid silver it was. Old man Zabowski gave us a dollar for it."

"Who's old man Zabowski?"

"A gent," answered the taller boy.

"Runs the pawnshop two blocks over," said the shorter one. "A real gent."

Arlie and Dwain and Noah had come up to stand beside Hugh. "Are we going to play ball?"

Hugh looked at the dark-skinned ones. They shrugged. "Name's Frank," said the taller one. "And this is my friend, Mario."

Hugh swept his arm out toward his brothers. "This here's

Arlie and this is Dwain and this is Noah. I'm Hugh. We ain't got a ball. We'll ask Zollie to get us one so's we won't have to use yours all the time."

For the first time Frank and Mario showed signs of friend-liness. Solemn and now with genuine kindliness they said, "We can all use our ball; it's a good one. But we never play till we've looked for valuables first. Until everybody's emptied their garbage and trash from the day before. They'll start coming pretty soon."

"Mrs. Haliki will be first," predicted Mario and all of the boys moved to the mattress and sat down on it and waited. A slight wind breezing through the alley lifted pieces of paper from the garbage cans and sent them swirling. The odor from the cans was thick and foul. Overhead the sky was pallid; a murky, smoke-cloud, palest yellow in the center and fringed in black, came lazily drifting across the tops of the buildings. It was early—only 8 A.M.

To Hugh the stains on the mattress looked like blood and he said so. Frank and Mario laughed. "Sure it's blood. Some-body died on it."

Hugh glanced at his brothers and moved away from the stain. "Who? Who died on it?"

Mario brushed his black bangs aside, looked up to the buildings on the opposite side of the alley and waved a hand. "Somebody who got hisself stabbed. It happens all the time here. People always fighting. Stabbing each other. This one was unlucky. He died."

Hugh stood up and away from the mattress. Frank's eyes, deep and gentle, followed him. He said, "It's nothing to be afraid of. Just a little ol' blood."

Hugh cleared his throat. "I was just wondering how old you

were. Arlie's four and Dwain's seven and Noah is nine and I'm ten. I was just wondering about you."

Frank absorbed himself with a loose button on his shirt. "I'm ten and Mario here is eleven," he said and then Mrs. Haliki came with two sacks of wet-looking garbage. She came out of her doorway and shuffled to the garbage cans. She did not look at the boys.

"Look how she walks," commented Mario. "Like a duck. Fat old duck. Fat old good for nothing."

Frank called out to the woman. "Good morning, Mrs. Haliki."

The woman turned and stared at them. She muttered something in a foreign tongue.

"You going to church this morning, Mrs. Haliki? Hey, you're spilling your garbage! You better pick it up, Mrs. Haliki. You know what Father Michael said, that we should keep this place clean."

Mrs. Haliki's slack mouth formulated a silent remark. Finished with the dumping of her sodden bundles, she wiped her hands on her skirt, turned, and shuffled off down the alley toward the street.

"Now she'll go to church," said Mario, "and get herself saved for today and then she'll go to work."

"Marvella might go to work tomorrow," offered Arlie.

Frank turned his bright, black gaze on the little boy. "Who's Marvella?"

Arlie slid a thumb into his mouth. "She's our sister. We going to play ball?"

"In a minute."

"What're we waiting for?"

"For the others to come out," replied Frank. "There are

about eight more and there might be valuables in what they throw out."

All of the boys sat on the mattress and waited and presently, one by one, the people came out of the doorways on the opposite side of the alley and deposited their garbage in the open, bulging cans. They were shoddy and sullen. Frank and Mario called out good morning to all of them but they said nothing in return. All of them went down the alley toward the street and the cloud of smoke overhead was joined by another and yet another.

Dwain was rubbing his eyes. "Something stinks," he complained.

"You'll get used to it," said Mario and he and Frank stood up and moved toward the garbage cans. They stood over them, shaking their heads. They looked to Mrs. Haliki's door and the narrow window next it and bent their heads close together, whispering. After a moment they came back to the mattress. They were smiling. They sat down. Frank had taken a knife from his pocket and was nipping at the dark, fragile hairs on his forearms, first the right and then the left, switching the knife back and forth from hand to hand. "Mrs. Haliki," he said, "has got a gold piece that belongs to us. We sure wish we had it."

The Proffitt children leaned forward. "A gold piece?"

"Solid gold. We found it and it's ours. But Mrs. Haliki, she made us give it to her. She said it was hers."

"Was it?"

"Of course not. She just said that to make us hand it over. She couldn't even tell us the date on it. If you had a gold piece, you'd know the date on it, wouldn't you?"

"Yes," said Hugh. "I would. Anybody would."

Frank put his knife away and flung his hair back. "She keeps it wrapped up in a box. Mario and me peeked in her window one night and caught her looking at it."

"It belonged to the man who got hisself stabbed," supplied Mario. "It rolled out of his pocket when they was carrying him out and Frank and me found it. But then that fat old duck Haliki started screaming her head off, yelling it was hers, that the stabbed guy had stole it from her and so, to shut her mouth up, we gave it to her."

"He was our friend," gently interposed Frank. "He was sick a lot and Mario and me used to go up to his room and set with him. He didn't have no family. Just us. We was the only ones ever went to see him."

"If you were his friend," said Hugh, slowly deciding, "and now he's dead and no family to claim the gold piece and you found it when it rolled out of his pocket then you should have it. Not Mrs. Haliki. Not that fat old duck."

"We could get it back," said Mario. "It wouldn't be any trick. All we'd have to do is go up to Mrs. Haliki's window— You see how close it is to the ground there?—and push it open and crawl in and get the gold piece and then crawl back out again. It wouldn't be any trick. The box she keeps it in is in the dresser in the kitchen."

"Except," said Frank in a soft, slurred voice, "both me and Mario are too big for the window. It'd take somebody little."

They were both looking at Hugh and he was looking back at them, these newfound friends. He had gotten used to the odor from the garbage cans and the queer, overhead smoke now. It was rather pleasant sitting out there on the stained mattress with his brothers and his new friends. True, the concrete alley wasn't anything like the lush, green playground they were accustomed to back in Goose Elk. There weren't any trees to climb except Marvella's imaginary ones and those didn't count, of course. In the wintertime when the snow came there wouldn't be any place to sled. There wouldn't be any pond or stream for ice skating. Still this place had its good points. The buildings for one thing were good. The buildings on both sides and in front and back of them were protection. In the tar-papered house in Goose Elk there wasn't any such protection. You just sat out there alone when the winds and the ice and the snow came and toughed it out. To keep warm at night you slept four in a bed and put off going to the outside toilet as long as you could. The pink apartment with the flush toilet was nice. In the winter they'd be able to laugh at the cold and the snow from its windows. There'd be heat. A big furnace in the basement of the building took care of that. There'd be plenty to eat. Zollie had already started her job—had gone off with Juanita to start it—and Marvella was going out after one, too. Oh, they wouldn't lack for anything. This Chicago was nice. These two new friends—Frank and Mario—were nice. That fat old Mrs. Haliki—that fat old duck—should be ashamed of herself, talking them out of their gold piece.

Hugh looked toward Mrs. Haliki's window and surprised himself by saying, "Arlie could get through it. 'Twouldn't be no trouble for him, he's so little."

Frank flung his hair back and looked hesitant. "Well," he said. "Well."

The bravery of his intention took hold of Hugh. "We could do it now. Everybody's gone, aren't they? Arlie could be in and out of there quick as a cat. Then you'd have your gold piece."

Mario's black eyes were sparkling. His full red lips parted

in a smile. He leaned and put his hand on Hugh's shoulder. "Good idea. A *good* idea. Me and Frank would never have thought of it. Good thinking, Hugh. You're a gent. A real gent."

CHAPTER THREE

At four o'clock in the afternoon Marvella looked from the window of the pink apartment and saw Zollie and Juanita coming up the alley. They had their arms linked and were laughing. They were eating something from a brown paper bag carried by Juanita.

She went down the back stairway which contained lost odors—dust and sour grease and a vague, flesh smell—and met them. They came up to the bottom step and Zollie eased herself down on it. Her hair was tumbled loose and she had chocolate on her mouth. She said her feet were killing her.

"Did you see about me having a job at the hotel?" Marvella asked.

"We asked," replied Juanita. "They wanted to know how old you were and like fools—before we thought—we told them the truth. So now that's out."

Zollie opened her big, imitation-leather handbag. Tucked inside there were twelve small bars of soap, all individually and fancily wrapped. "Look," she said. "We're never gonna have to buy any more soap. They got tons of it. I never saw so much soap or so much toilet paper or so many towels. Tomorrow I'm gonna start layin' us in a supply of towels and wash rags."

Juanita was unscrewing the pearl bobs in her ears. "So the hotel job is out for you but I saw Mr. Zabowski in the bakery just now. He needs somebody to help him in his store while his family's gone to Europe. Why don't you just run over there and see him now?"

"Who's Mr. Zabowski?" asked Marvella.

Juanita dropped the earbobs into her purse. "He runs a pawnshop two blocks over from here. Just go down to the end of the alley and turn to your left and keep going. You'll run into it. There's a big sign in his window says Zabowski."

"Should I tell him how old I am?"

"He knows already," answered Juanita. "We told him. To him it doesn't make any difference."

The little kids were way down at the far end of the alley playing ball with the two dark-skinned children. Marvella went out into the alley and walked its length and entered the street and was immediately caught up in a human stream. There were so many people and they all seemed crazily intent on going in the same direction as herself. She met their glassy stares and a small, uncertain convulsion took place in her mind. Back in Goose Elk people on the streets looked pleasant and spoke to each other. These people looked like they were mad. Some of them looked scared. They were rude. A black-faced man wearing a pink helmet crashed sideways into her and didn't apologize. At the corner where there was a traffic light she caught up with him. He slitted his eyes and glanced down at her but didn't speak. The color of the traffic light changed and she was swept along in a jostle and a push to the opposite curb. There were planes in the sky. The air was bright. She stood on the curb and waited for the light to change again.

The tall buildings had claimed the landscape and the sky. There was not a sprig of natural greenery anywhere—just mile upon mile of glass and concrete and swarming people—an endless vista of deadly efficiency and deafening confusion.

If all the birds in North Carolina were suddenly to come and set themselves down here in the middle of this street, she thought, it wouldn't make one bit of difference. If they screeched their lungs out, all together, nobody'd hear them.

Mr. Zabowski's window sign was magnificent—all rich, dark gold edged in gleaming black. She peered through the letters of it and saw what was inside: long, wall-shelves containing cameras, guitars with mother-of-pearl fronts, small silver radios, watches with gem-studded bands, trays of rings sparkling icy white against black velvet. There was a counter and behind it there was a man. He was counting money from a drawer.

She left the window and went to the door of the shop and pushed on it and went inside.

The man behind the counter glanced up, grabbed a folded sheet of newspaper, covered the money, said, "Yes? Something?"

"I'm Marvella Proffitt," she said. "My aunt said for me to come see you about helping you in your store."

Mr. Zabowski's pale eyelids fluttered. "Oh. Well, I be with you in one minute. Just slide the bolt on the door there, hey?

So nobody else comes in. I will be through here in one minute and then we will talk."

At Mr. Zabowski's invitation she sat on a stool back of the counter and watched him count the money from the drawer. It was more than she had ever seen all at one time before.

Mr. Zabowski's short, squat legs were lost in his brown, baggy trousers. His fat little feet in brown scuffed shoes moved back and forth and sideways as he laid the bills from the drawer out flat, smoothing them with his thumb, and stacked the coins in neat denominational piles.

The air in the shop was cool and close. She forced herself to breathe it evenly. If she got the job how much money would she make? With her first pay she'd buy everybody a present. Each of the little kids and Pa. And Zollie. Maybe Juanita.

Mr. Zabowski had finished his counting. Now he was writing down on a long slip of paper how much. His tongue was at the corner of his mouth. He was smiling to himself.

He's glad he has all that money, thought Marvella. We've never had enough. That's because we don't know things. All our lives we've never known anything except Goose Elk and living in a shack on the side of a mountain and raising hogs and beating our brains out trying to grub a living from the fields. Them blasted hogs and them blasted fields. Back home in Goose Elk, right this very minute, the Critchers would be out in the fields, the littlest ones running on ahead of the plows, reveling in the black dirt and the sun and each other. Mr. Critcher would be bawling to them to get out of the way, his voice carrying out across the hollow, down across the sunken meadows, brilliant in summer color, and they wouldn't be paying any attention to him. They'd be laughing. Above the hollow, spreading away to the ridges and the peaks surrounding it, there would be long white drifts of pure, shining clouds. The birds would be there, hopping around among the grass and wildflower clumps, smacking and chittering.

Them Critchers, thought Marvella. Them hog poisoners. Someday we're going to go back there. Not to stay—just for a visit. We're going to go back there in style. *Big style.* In a new car. And new clothes. And lots of money in our pockets. I'll get Pa a suit and a hat to match. I'll put a twenty-dollar bill in his pocket and let the edge of it stick out just enough to show. I'll say I thought it was a handkerchief—that I put it there by mistake. Mr. Critcher's eyeballs will fall out.

Someone was at the shop door, rattling the outside catch. Mr. Zabowski drew a total to the column of figures on his sheet, took a cloth bag from beneath the counter, scooped all the money into it. "Everybody wants something from Zabowski," he said. "Go see who it is. Tell them I'm closed for the day. Tell them to come back tomorrow."

Marvella slipped from her stool, went to the door and slid the bolt. The two dark-skinned children from the alley pushed in. "Mr. Zabowski's closed for the day," she said. "Come back tomorrow."

They grinned at her, pushed past her, and trotted over to the counter and leaned on it, looking up at Mr. Zabowski. "Got something for youse," the taller one drawled.

Mr. Zabowski had stuck the bag of money beneath the counter. The slight exertion from doing this, from bending over, had reddened his smooth, round face. He straightened and looked at the boys. "Oh, hello, Frank. Hello, Mario. What have you got for me?"

Frank took a coin from his pocket and laid it on the counter. His black eyes were lazy. "Pure gold, Mr. Zabowski. How much'll you give us for it?"

Mr. Zabowski glanced at the coin. He shrugged. "Fifty cents maybe."

The one named Mario put his hands to his head and dragged his hair down over his eyes. The expression in his eyes, peering out through the dark, glossy strands, gently chided Mr. Zabowski. "You're a card, Mr. Zabowski. A real card. Didn't you hear what Frank said? This here is pure gold. Come on now. How much?"

Mr. Zabowski fluttered his pale lids. "Where did you get it?"

The boy named Frank took a knife from his pocket, flicked the blade open, began nipping at the soft hair-fuzz on his forearms. "We found it in the alley."

"I'll give you a dollar for it," said Mr. Zabowski.

"It's gold," said Frank.

"I'll give you two dollars for it," said Mr. Zabowski. "Take it or leave it."

Frank stuck his hand out and Mario laughed. Mr. Zabowski leaned and, after fiddling with the money bag under the counter for a second or two, produced two one-dollar bills. Solemnly he slid them across the counter and Frank picked them up and pocketed them. Mario was still laughing. Frank took him by the arm and they skipped out, banging the door behind them.

Mr. Zabowski went to the door and again bolted it. He came back to the counter, picked up the gold piece and slipped it into his pocket. "Now then," he said. "I have been thinking about you working for me. I could not pay you much, you understand, because there is not much work. Just a little dusting and to stay here when I go to the bank and for my lunch. Not to do any trading with anybody, you understand."

Lifted toward safety, carried into the delight of this unexpected good fortune, Marvella clasped her hands behind her back. "Yes, sir."

"I will tell people," said Mr. Zabowski, "that you are my protégée. That way we won't either one get into no trouble."

She wondered what a portegee was. She said, "Yes, sir. That sounds fair enough."

"Or better yet," said Mr. Zabowski, "I will tell them you are my niece. What's the name of that place in North Carolina where you come from?"

"Goose Elk."

Mr. Zabowski gazed at her. "Goose Elk. Funny name. What's there?"

"Nothing much. A general store. Some churches. A school."

"You go to school?"

"I did last year. This year I don't reckon I will. We're broke now."

Mr. Zabowski moved his colorless eyelids up and down.

In her new importance Marvella explained. "The Critchers, the people who live in the holler down below our place, poisoned all our hogs and then we got a blight in our fields that killed off all our crops. Zollie got the county farm man—the government man—to come and take a sample of the dirt and say what it was but he never came back to let us know. Then Zollie got mad and said she was through with the whole mess. Then we packed up all our stuff and left and came here."

Mr. Zabowski had taken the gold piece from his pocket,

was thoughtfully looking at it. "Zollie sounds like she might have a little bit of a temper," he murmured.

"She has when she gets riled. When people try to cross her. She told the deputy sheriff that came out to see about our poisoned hogs to get off our property and stay off. You should've seen him run. His feet didn't hit the ground no more'n twice between the pigsty and his car. Zollie had Pa's shotgun and it was loaded and she plain meant for him to get off our property and stay off. She would've blowed his head off if Pa hadn't stopped her. Zollie's mean when she's riled. Last year we made some dandelion wine and Zollie got drunk on it and took a can of gasoline and went down to the Critchers' place and poured it on their bedroom window and struck a match to it. It didn't hurt anything; it was just on the glass part of the window. But old man Critcher nearly broke the door down getting out of there. Zollie was laughing so hard she forgot to run and then she and Mr. Critcher had a fight. She laid her right fist side of his head so hard he couldn't hear it thunder for a week. Then Mrs. Critcher came tromping up the hill, a-yelling what all she was going to do to us and her and me had it. I *mean* we flat had it. She hit Arlie—he's my littlest brother— and I mean I flat crawled all over her. I doubt she knew what hit her. Her young-uns had to come after her. She knocked one of my teeth out. See? See this one gone? Mrs. Critcher did it."

Mr. Zabowski tilted forward for a look. "Lucky for you it's not a front one. Usually when people get teeth knocked out it's in the front. From the side it don't show so much being gone."

"She really walloped me."

Mr. Zabowski returned the gold coin in his pocket. "Yes. Well, here in Chicago we don't have any people like that. No gangsters like that. Just good kind, honest people. You come tomorrow morning nine o'clock, hey?"

"Yes, sir!" answered Marvella. "I'll be here tomorrow morning at nine o'clock sharp!"

Going home, going back to the pink apartment, she felt like a conquering queen. Now the world seemed brilliantly friendly. It was just dusk but already the emblazoned night lights were beginning to wink and glow. Beneath them the great city howled and growled and murmured and squeaked. There was the wind and the babel of foreign tongues and the sound of her own footsteps, quick on the pavement.

When the night had settled down over the alley there came from one of the dimly lighted doorways across the way a piercing shriek. "Police! Police! I've been robbed! Somebody call the police!"

Dorman Proffitt raised his head and said, "What's that?" And Juanita, who had suppered with them, answered, "It's nothing. Just that crazy Haliki woman again. Is there any more tea, Zollie?"

Zollie poured more cold tea over Juanita's ice cubes and the little kids, one by one, left their chairs and went to the front room to assemble around the television set.

The shrieking across the alley ceased as abruptly as it had started. Marvella helped her father find his way from his supper chair to the one in the corner of the front room. "My eyes is a-paining me," he complained. "I wisht I could see but I reckon there's not much chance in that a-coming unless the Lord sees fit to do a miracle on me."

"Pa," said Marvella. "You need to see a doctor. That one back home might've been wrong to say there wasn't any hope. All of your sight didn't go until just a year ago. Maybe it could be made to come back. I think we should take you to another doctor and see."

Her father began to knead his knees. "No money for that now. Doctors cost money."

"We've got money, Pa. We've got forty dollars left in our savings and Zollie's making good money at her job and now I've got one, too."

"How much," asked her father, "is Mr. Zabowski going to pay you?"

"I don't know, Pa. I forgot to ask him. But it'll be fair whatever it is. Tomorrow I'll ask Mr. Zabowski to give me the name of a good doctor. He'll know one."

Her father's mouth grew peaked. He released his sigh. "We'll see. After you've worked a while we'll see. Tell me again what it looks like out there. Any sign of rain? It hasn't rained since we've been here. The trees, they don't stay healthy without rain."

She went past the little kids, huddled raptly around the television set. She looked out the window and saw a white car with a winking light on its top pulling into the alley. It stopped before Mrs. Haliki's doorway and two uniformed men got out of it. They went inside. She turned her head and concentrated and into her mind there came the picture of her imagined trees, billowing palest green in the eerie night light. The mimosa tree, standing out from the others, was drenched in a luxuriant mist, its lovely, feather-shaped leaves drooped with the cool moisture. Now beneath its protective spread there were shocks of fiddlehead fern and foot-high grass interspersed with the white, star-shaped blooms of chickweed and delicately colored orchises. The waves of the blue mountain ridges spread out grandly at its back.

She went back to her father. "There's no sight of rain, Pa, but there's a heavy fog like we have back home. The trees look healthy."

Her father said, "Eh law," and put his head back and closed his eyes. U. S. 1818775

Sprawled on the floor in front of the television set, Arlie had fallen asleep. Marvella picked him up and carried him back to the room the little kids shared. Hugh followed her. He watched her remove Arlie's shoes and socks. He said, "Uh, Marvella, I think I got to tell you something."

"In a minute," she said, stuffing Arlie's limp, naked body into pajamas.

Hugh chewed his lower lip. "This morning," he said, "this morning we did something maybe we shouldn't ought to have done. This morning it was all right. I thought it was. But now I'm scared."

"Of what, Hugh?"

"Of . . . I don't know. I don't like it here."

"That's too bad. You'll get used to it though. It's nothing to be a-scared of."

Miserably Hugh looked at her. "That's not it. This morning . . . Well, you know Frank and Mario?"

"Frank and Mario. No. Wait a minute. Yes. Frank and Mario. They came into Mr. Zabowski's shop while I was there talking to him about my job. They sold him a gold piece they'd found for two dollars."

Hugh licked his lips and turned his face from her. "They didn't find it, Marvella. Not like they prob'ly told old man

Zabowski they did. It was theirs but . . . A sick man they was friends to . . . It rolled out of his pocket the night he got stabbed and they found it. But then Mrs. Haliki yelled her head off, claiming it was hers, claiming the man who was stabbed had stole it from her. And so Frank and Mario had to hand it over to her. To make her stop yelling her head off about it."

"Hugh," said Marvella. "Hugh, what are you trying to say?"

Hugh dragged his fingers through his yellow hair. On a note of desperate anxiety he began to whisper: "I'm trying to tell you what happened this morning. We was all out in the alley playing ball. Frank and Mario was there. And they told us about the gold piece, how old Mrs. Haliki got it away from them. They said they could get it back easy but they was too big to go through Mrs. Haliki's window. So I said let Arlie go. He's little. And so then we waited till everybody had gone off to work and then we lifted Arlie up and pushed him through the window and he went in and got the gold piece and came back out again."

Marvella had drawn back from her brother. She was staring at him. She too began to whisper. "Oh, Hugh. But that's . . . that's stealing!"

Hugh sunk his chin. "It didn't seem like it then. It seemed all right this morning. It was my idea. Mario even thanked me for having it. Nobody can tell . . . I had Arlie take his shoes off. He was careful not to leave any sign. Frank wiped the windowsill afterward. But now . . . now I'm afraid. The law's over at Mrs. Haliki's. Maybe they'll come over here. To ask questions. I can't . . . What if they find out it was Arlie? It wasn't really. He was just the one to go in. I told him to. It was my idea but now . . . now if they make me tell . . . What will they do to Arlie? And me?"

A pulse had begun to beat against Marvella's brain. This was bad business. The law here wouldn't be like the law back in Goose Elk—one man just piddle-diddling with it when he got time. Instinct told her that. Instinct told her that here it would be serious. There wouldn't be any dawdling around with it—no threat for next time. The law back in Goose Elk never arrested anybody unless pushed to it. People could even poison other people's hogs and they wouldn't get arrested. Here it would be different. Arlie was just a baby; so was Hugh for that matter. But maybe the law wouldn't look on them as babies. Another thought siezed her. Frank and Mario had sold the coin to Mr. Zabowski. Mightn't that get *him* into trouble? It might. Then where would *she* be? Out of a job, that's where. Jobs didn't grow on trees. Not for somebody fourteen years old. Mr. Zabowski understood and was going to help her but who else would do the same?

Marvella put the tip of her tongue in the tooth-hole and felt the weight of her hair and was conscious of the pulse beating against her brain. It stopped.

Hugh was looking at her, worrying his lip with his teeth and pulling at his hair, waiting for her to relieve him of his terrible worry.

She said, "Hugh, when the police come—if they come— you aren't to say anything. You don't know anything. It didn't happen. Just get it fixed in your mind that it didn't happen. Can you do that?"

Gravely Hugh regarded her. "Yes. I think so."

"You'll *have* to do it, Hugh. There's no other way. Don't you understand? We came here to live, not get ourselves in trouble right off. It wasn't . . . Don't you see? Maybe the gold piece *did* belong to Frank and Mario. But anyway, Mr.

Zabowski has it now. He bought it from Frank and Mario. Don't you see?"

Hugh dropped his hands. "Yes, I see. All right."

Her head felt wobbly. She said, "Go out now and send Noah and Dwain in here. Don't make any fuss about it. We don't want Zollie or Pa or Juanita to know about this."

CHAPTER FOUR

The police came, treading heavily up the dark steps, and Zollie went to answer their knock. The little kids sat in front of the television set, watching the picture on its screen. Hugh had hunched himself closer to the box than the others. He sat tensely, trying to remember not to pull his hair or worry his lip. The police would notice him doing these things and he didn't want to be noticed. His fingers were trembling and he shoved his hands into his pockets. He was conscious of an intense thirst.

Zollie was at the door talking with the two policemen. Big and brash and ready to fight, she was saying, "Yes, we just moved here. Our name is Proffitt. That man over there is my husband, that woman over there is my sister, this big girl here is my daughter, them's my boys. That's all of us except the baby. He's asleep."

One of the men asked a low, polite question and Zollie laughed. "A gold piece? What's that? I ain't *never* seen no gold piece. You want to come in and search us for it? Is that what you want?"

Both men were shorter than Zollie and smaller. They had to step around her to get a look at the room and what was in it. They said, "We'd just like to ask the boys a few questions."

Standing beside Marvella, Juanita said, "You got a search warrant?"

The policemen were patient. "We just want to ask the little boys a question or two."

In his chair in the corner, Dorman Proffitt had leaned forward, was trying to grasp the situation. "What is it, Zollie? What's going on? Is they some trouble?"

As if he were deaf instead of blind, Zollie shouted her answer. "No trouble, Dorman! It's just the police a-wanting to ask the boys some questions!"

"I wouldn't allow it," muttered Juanita. "I'd make 'em go and get a search warrant."

"Just a couple of questions," the police said. "That's all."

Abruptly Zollie gave in. She shrugged. "All right, help yourself. But hurry it up. We got other things to do with our time."

The two policemen walked over to the little boys and squatted beside them. Hugh reached up and pushed the button on the television set. The picture on its screen faded.

It didn't happen, thought Hugh. That's all I've got to remember. That it didn't happen. He made himself look at the policemen. Ever so quietly, being friendly and nice, they started their questions and he and Dwain and Noah answered them:

"We played ball all day. In the alley."

"Just the three of you?"

"No. Arlie, too. He's just four so doesn't count though."

"Anybody else?"

"There was Frank and Mario."

The policemen exchanged looks. "Yes, we know about Frank and Mario. We've already talked with them. Did you see anybody strange in the alley? While you were playing?"

"Everybody was strange. We never saw any of 'em before. We've just come here from Goose Elk, North Carolina."

"The people we saw live in the house on the other side of the alley," supplied Dwain. "They was going to work when we saw them. We watched them and then we played ball."

"We sat on the mattress that's down there," explained Noah. "There's blood spots on it and Frank said a man got hisself stabbed on it. Frank's nice. He's a . . . a gent."

"A real gent," echoed Dwain.

Hugh's palms were wet and the thirst in his throat hurt. The policemen were both looking at him intently. Because I'm the oldest they expect me to say the most, he thought. To make it all clear. He swallowed and the words came out in a gentle, little puff. "We didn't do anything we weren't supposed to do. All we did was play ball. All morning we just played ball. At dinner time we all came up here and ate some sandwiches Zollie'd made for us and then we went back again and played some more. And that's all."

"These kids never lie," said Zollie in a grand, prideful way.

"That Haliki woman is slightly bats," muttered Juanita. "It's always something with her. You two fellas should know that by now. You've been around here often enough, checking up on her crazy complaints."

The policemen rose. They were apologetic. They walked toward the door. Zollie opened it for them. They went down the steps. Juanita snorted.

Hugh reached up and pulled the knob on the television set. Noah and Dwain turned their faces to it. Hugh got up and went to the kitchen and drank four glasses of water.

In the alley rats investigated the garbage. Among that deposited by Mrs. Haliki they found a bone with bits of gristle clinging to it.

It was July so that the morning light came early, sliding down over the tops of the buildings, glinting the windows along the alley, slowly advancing and settling until all of the strip was bathed in clear sparkling sunshine.

The little kids sat on the mattress and soberly watched the people come out of the buildings and go down the alley and enter the street. This morning Mrs. Haliki was the last. She looked at them with her great, popping eyes but didn't speak. The hem of her skirt was ripped loose in the back.

"Fat old duck," said Noah.

They didn't speak of the happenings of the night before. They sat on the mattress and waited for Frank and Mario and presently they came. Frank had a double handful of white grapes. Mario was eating a long chocolate-covered confection that oozed. Both had on their clothes of the day before. They capered up and down stuffing the grapes and the oozy thing into their mouths. Frank said that they might go to a movie as soon as it opened up.

Hugh looked at him. "The police was over to our place last night."

Frank spit grape seeds. "Yeah? What'd youse tell 'em?"

"Nothing."

"Wasn't nothing to tell, was there?"

"No."

"They came up and talked to Mario and me, too," said

42

Frank. " 'Course we couldn't tell them anything either. There wasn't nothing to tell."

Mario had finished his confection. He wiped his mouth on the sleeve of his shirt. He started to walk around in a slow circle.

Frank watched him. "You feel all right, Mario?"

Mario didn't answer. There was something wrong with him. Now he was zigzagging, totally absorbed in the movement of his feet, holding his head with both hands. He was breathing fast and grunting. The veins in his forehead had swelled and turned purple. He began to weave crazily.

Frank stuffed all of his remaining grapes into his mouth at one time, went to Mario, took his arm. "You'd better come lay down, Mario. Lay down on the mattress for a minute."

A thick, shiny foam had started to come from Mario's mouth and flecks of blood from his nose. He was moaning and trying to shake Frank's hand off. Frank was dragging him toward the mattress. "You're going to have one of your fits, Mario. Lay down for a minute. You *got* to lay down. If you don't you'll hurt yourself. There. Lay there. It's all right, it's all right."

Arlie had his thumb in his mouth. He was crooning to himself and watching Mario. Noah and Dwain and Hugh had fearfully risen from the mattress. Hugh asked, "What is it? What's the matter with him?"

"He has fits," replied Frank. "Has anybody got . . . I need . . . something to put in his mouth. To keep him from swallowing his tongue. A handkerchief or a stick. Anything."

Noah came out of his fright. He darted over to the garbage cans, frantically searched, found a rag, seized it, came running back. "Will this do?"

Frank, without looking at it, made a twisted rope of the rag and stuffed it into Mario's mouth. He pulled Mario's tongue out. "Hold his feet," he directed in a calm voice.

Noah and Dwain went to Mario's feet and held them down. Frank was trying to capture Mario's flailing arms. "Help me," he said to Hugh. "No, not like that, stupid. Hold his wrist and his elbow. He'll break something if you don't. Hold his arm, stupid! You want him to punch his eye out?"

Mario's body was stiff and arched. The blood was spurting out of his nose. He jerked up and down and back and forth. His swollen tongue was purple and his eyes rolled and heaved. He seemed to Hugh to be caught in some unendurable agony. He held on to Mario's arm by the wrist and elbow. "Shouldn't we call somebody?" he gasped. "A grown-up? His mother? Where's his mother?"

Frank was holding on to his calm. His black hair was flung down over his eyes. He was holding on to Mario, watching closely and counting. "One, two, three, four, five, six, seven, eight."

"Shouldn't we call his mother?" cried Hugh. "His mother should be here to do something!"

Frank didn't answer the question. He was being business-like. "Help me turn him on his side. If we don't turn him on his side he'll drown in his own blood."

Noah and Dwain and Hugh helped Frank turn Mario on to his side. The convulsion was over. Now he was limp and white. Frank took the rag out of Mario's mouth and wiped some of the blood away.

"He'll sleep now," said Frank. "It was just one of his fits. He'll be all right pretty soon. This was just a little one; only lasted eight minutes."

Everybody sat on the mattress and watched Mario. The crisis had passed.

44

"He's strong," commented Hugh. "What causes him to have fits? Why didn't we call his mother or is she one of the ones gone off to work?"

Frank flung his hair back. "Wouldn't have done any good to call his mother. She's asleep. She's always asleep. Anyway she doesn't care. I'm the only one that cares."

"But she's his mother," argued Hugh. "Even if she's asleep she'll want to know. We should go and tell her."

"Should huh?"

"Yes."

"Then you be the one," said Frank. "I'll wait here and watch Mario. It's just through the door over there and up two flights. Last apartment on the right. She'll be asleep so don't knock. Just go in and shake her and tell her about Mario. I'll wait for you here."

Hugh hesitated. There was something in Frank's manner that wasn't quite . . . quite honest. "Do you live up there, too?" he asked.

Frank made an irritated gesture with his hands and head. "Of course."

"You should be the one to tell Mario's mother," insisted Hugh. "I don't know her. She might think . . . something."

Frank said, "Aw, for cripe's sake," but stood up. "All right. I'll go with you but I'm telling you we'll be wasting our time. She won't do anything."

Frank in the lead, the two boys trotted across the alley and entered the doorway and went up the stairs. They reached the second floor and Frank sprinted down the dim, bare corridor, whacking on the doors lightly with his fist. From one of these a woman looked out after the door whacking. Hugh heard the door open and stopped and looked back.

Frank stopped, too, and turned around. He and the woman regarded each other.

"My mother," Frank said to Hugh. "Isn't she gorgeous?"

The woman fussed with the collar of her soiled, flowered wrapper. Her eyes were unfriendly. "Faugh," she said.

Hugh said, "What?"

Frank laughed. "It's her favorite word. She picked it up from a guy from England or Scotland or somewhere. Some bum she used to know. It just means she's disgusted; she always is." He smiled at his mother. "Mario's had another fit. I just came up to tell his mother. Hugh here thinks she might be interested. You think she might?"

"Faugh," said Frank's mother and retreated back into her apartment and slammed the door.

Mario's mother was asleep as Frank had said she would be. They entered her apartment without knocking and went in and stood beside her bed. The room was airless and dark. A tightly tacked blanket covered the single window. Clothes dangled from every knob. There was the smell of garlic and things that hadn't been washed.

"She keeps it nice, don't she?" said Frank, not asking a question.

Hugh was having a little trouble breathing. The smell was making him a little sick.

Frank bent over Mario's mother. "Woman. Woman. Wake up, woman."

The woman opened her large, clear eyes but didn't move. She lay perfectly motionless. "Oh, it's you, Frank."

"Yeh. Mario's just had another fit and Hugh here thought you might like to know about it. You c'n go back to sleep now. It ain't anything for you to worry about. Just a little ol' fit. Only lasted eight minutes."

Mario's mother closed her eyes again. "The doctor," she said. "The doctor should do something for Mario. It's what he gets paid for. But he don't know anything. He don't know as much as I do. Mario needs to be in the country where he can get some fresh air and have a horse. I told the doctor that but he don't listen. Them county people are all alike. They get paid to do a job but they don't do it. I don't know what to do about Mario. I'm sick myself."

"You should rest," suggested Frank.

"Yes."

"Just rest. There's nothin' for you to get up for anyway. Mario needs any looking out for I'll do it. You just lay here and rest."

"Yes."

"Mario's okay. It was just one of his little ol' fits. He ain't dead."

"Yes."

"You need anything?"

"Yes."

"I'll have it delivered," said Frank. "Should I tell them to charge it?"

"Yes," answered Mario's mother. She was asleep.

Frank and Hugh stood looking down at Mario's mother. It's something I don't understand, thought Hugh. These people are just different from us. If one of us was sick and needed to go to the country where we could have fresh air and a horse Zollie'd get us there. Marvella'd help her. This room isn't fitten for a hog to live in. So dirty and no air. No wonder she sleeps all the time. She does it so she won't have to look at it.

Going back down the hall toward the stairs Frank banged

hard on all the doors. On his mother's he banged hardest of all and kicked it and yelled, "Faugh!"

There was no reply from the other side.

They reached the first landing and Frank paused on it to turn and say, "If Mario asks, we'll tell him his mother cried. That'll make him feel better."

"Yes," agreed Hugh. "Yes, that's a good idea."

Until noon Mario lay on the mattress in the alley, sometimes awake, most of the time asleep. He complained of being sick to his stomach and Frank went after ice cream. Without much appetite Mario ate it and slept again.

Dwain and Noah and Arlie went upstairs for their noon sandwiches. Hugh said he wasn't hungry. He and Frank sat on the mattress and watched Mario.

The floe of yellow, oily clouds over the building tops moved sluggishly. They were artificial and therefore nature wasn't having too much to do with them.

Frank had built Mario a tent out of newspaper to shield his face from the sun. He lay with his knees drawn up, one hand under his cheek, breathing evenly.

"He's sick," said Frank. "And somebody should do something about it. Only there ain't anybody. You saw his mother."

Hugh sighed. Something deep in him spoke for him. "It prob'ly isn't her fault. She prob'ly doesn't have any money."

"Money," said Frank. "Everything's money. Why is that?"

"I don't know, Frank."

Frank flung his long, black hair back. "I do. It's the way grown-ups have fixed it. I don't like it and I'm going to do something about it. Just as soon as Mario gets over this. There's people living in other parts of this town that don't even know we're here. You ever stop to think about that?"

48

"No, Frank."

"Well, there is. There's people living in other parts of this town that . . . that eat meat every day and wear different clothes every day and get to go to the doctor when they're sick. A paid doctor. Not a county one where they shove you around. That's the kind of doctor Mario needs. One that gets paid so he'll be interested in what's wrong with him. I hate them county doctors like dirt. Every time you go you have to explain it all again because they're new each time and by the time you get it all said your turn is up and still nothing's been done."

Above them the artificial yellow clouds suddenly moved. A gaseous odor from them drifted down into the alley. Hugh breathed the odor and coughed and looked at Frank. He felt powerless. Back home in Goose Elk the Proffitts had had their problems all right with Pa going blind and the Critchers always wanting to fight and then the poisoned hogs and the blighted fields. But this was something different. This was something you couldn't get ahold of. Doctors were supposed to help people whether you had the money to pay them or not. They were supposed to listen and help people. Dr. Winebarger did, back in Goose Elk. Somebody should speak to the doctor that Mario went to and tell him . . . Tell him what? To sit still and listen? And help? How could you tell a doctor that? If he didn't know to do that already how could you tell him? This county doctor who wasn't interested?

Frank had his knife out but wasn't using it on anything. He had his eyes half-shut. On his face there was a cold, passionate look. "Tomorrow I'm going out and get some money," he said. "I'm gonna go to the Loop."

"What's the Loop?"

"Hillbilly."

"Well, what is it?"

"It's where the elevated trains are. And the business. All the stores and the hotels. People. There are always lots of people there."

"And somebody there is going to give you some money?"

"Hillbilly."

"Well?"

Frank leaned over and adjusted the newspaper tent that covered Mario's face. He straightened. Earnestly and honestly he spoke. "Nobody's going to give me anything. I'm going to steal it. I know how. I've seen other guys do it. It ain't hard. You got to be quick is all. And don't lose your head. And don't panic. Get the money out quick and then get rid of it quick."

"Get rid of what quick?"

Frank was silent for a long moment. He put the knife away and rubbed his arms. He sighed. "I'm talking about snatching somebody's purse tomorrow, stupid. That's what I'm talking about. That's where I'm going to get money tomorrow. It's to help Mario. If I don't help him he'll die."

Strangely Hugh was not shocked. What Frank was talking about had no connection with him. This Loop, where all the business and people and stores and hotels were, had no connection with him. He didn't want to hear about Frank's plans concerning money. He had had enough trouble with himself over the gold piece. Guilt wasn't such an easy thing to get shed of. He had had enough of crime. It was plain to see that Mario did need help. Somebody should help him. But it should be a grown-up. Mario's mother or the county doctor. Some grown-up. Frank shouldn't have to be the one. He didn't want to hear about what Frank had planned.

Frank was looking at him. "How about you going with me?"

Hugh shook his head. "No."

"Why not?"

"Because I don't want to."

"It's for Mario, Hugh. You don't want him to die, do you?"

"Of course not."

"Then go with me."

"No. You might get caught. Besides it isn't . . . Grown-ups should be the ones to do. Not just you. By yourself."

"Grown-ups don't care. Not the ones I know."

Hugh turned his head and looked at Mario's feet. "His father prob'ly does. Where's his father?"

Frank laughed. "Who's got a father?"

"Hasn't Mario?"

"No."

"Haven't you?"

"No."

Deeply troubled, Hugh sat and looked at his new friend and the garbage cans and Mario's feet and the bloodstains on the mattress. Mario's blood, spilling from his nose, had made more of them.

CHAPTER FIVE

Marvella was sweeping the sidewalk outside Mr. Zabowski's store and watching the pedestrian traffic. The older people, drooping and shambling along, stayed close to the buildings. They were not interested in what was in the windows; they didn't look at each other. At the bus stop, midway in the street, they gathered together in a little cluster but each stood in separate silence. There were slivers of dust in the wind and these and the heat touched their dejected faces.

Two young girls, carrying themselves tall and straight, came out of a building and stood on the curb. They swung their white purses and sauntered up and down and kept looking at their watches. The wind lifted the skirts of their thin, bright dresses and they pretended embarrassment. They smoothed their skirts and tossed their fluffy heads, and walked up and down. Their legs were shapely and Marvella thought they might be pleased to show them off. With her broom she gave the sidewalk a final lick and went back inside the store.

Mr. Zabowski was on his stool behind the counter reading a foreign newspaper and drinking hot tea from a tall glass. Without looking up he said, "Dust now but don't flap. There is a rag on the table behind the curtain there. Damp it a little first."

She went behind the curtain and found the rag. She went to the sink in the corner and held the rag under the single tap, wetting it. This back room was very untidy. There was a cot with a rumpled cotton blanket and a limp pillow, a hot plate with a frayed cord, a soiled towel hanging on a nail, a small table over-burdened with soiled dishes. The water coming from the tap smelled like medicine. She wrung the rag until it was almost dry and went back out into the main room of the store. Two policemen had come in but not to pawn or buy anything. They were slouched at the counter thumbing through one of Mr. Zabowski's ledgers.

Explaining Marvella, Mr. Zabowski said, "This is my niece. She is helping me out until my wife and daughter get back from Europe."

Trim and impersonal, the two men merely glanced at Marvella. Finished with the ledger, they closed it and said, "See you tomorrow," and left.

Wiping dust from the shelves, Marvella asked, "Do they come every day?"

Mr. Zabowski nodded. "Yes."

"What're they looking for?"

"Thieves."

"What thieves?"

"Just thieves. Don't flap, please. I have allergy."

Marvella moved a clock and wiped dust without flapping. "I think it would be terrible to be a thief. I wonder what makes one."

Mr. Zabowski fluttered his pale eyelids. "Who knows? Different people have different reasons for being what they are."

"Yes, but to be a thief. I think that'd be pretty bad. You'd always have to be worrying about getting caught and going to jail. I wonder why thieves just don't work for what they want. It's a lot more simple."

"Some people don't like work," observed Mr. Zabowski.

Marvella laughed. "That's crazy. Work's good for the soul. Pa started teaching me that when I was just a little kid. Every one of my little brothers has been taught that too. We've got two rules we go by: Work when there's work to be done and go by the Golden Rule. Pa says if a person goes by just those two things he won't ever have anything to worry about."

"I think you have a good, wise parent," said Mr. Zabowski. He left his stool and went to the door of the shop. He was sneezing. Now the stream of foot traffic on the street outside had diminished. Weak currents of wind riffled paper and other debris in the gutters. The earlier sun had gone; the sky above the buildings was slowly turning a gunmetal gray. Blows of thunder in other, distant parts of the city boomed.

Mr. Zabowski came back to the counter, went behind it and locked the cash drawer. "I don't feel so good," he said. "Anybody comes I'll be in the back room. Just shake me; I wake up quick."

Marvella dusted the shelves and after this was finished sat on the stool and looked out through the open door to the street. After a while the gunmetal sky lowered and big drops of rain fell. She saw one of the dark-skinned boys from the alley—the one named Frank—go by. He had on a too-big canvas raincoat and was hurrying.

This day exhausted her. She sat on the stool and listened to Mr. Zabowski's sleep sounds coming from the back room. He groaned and snored and every time he turned on his cot it creaked. The wind blew the rain in and she made the decision to close the street door. She sat on the stool and watched the rain wash the window. No customers came. At noon she ate the sandwich and cookies she had brought from home. Mr. Zabowski came from the back room and went around turning on lights. "Is a bad day for business," he commented and went back to his cot.

In the street water overflowed the gutters. Buses lumbered by and their whirling tires sprayed the air. People with umbrellas went past. Marvella sat in the warm, damp, gloomy dusk of the shop and thought about Goose Elk, how it looked during a rainstorm; the thunderheads boiling black along the mountain crowns and the wind-filled rain pouring down in great, cold blasts. Back home storms didn't fool around. They boomed across the ridges and hollows like cannons. They lashed at the trees and laid the meadows flat. They loosened great rocks and sent them crashing. Everything, during one of these, ran for cover. Lightning could kill and falling rock could kill and if you had any sense you would stay inside until it was over. Here it was different. This rain was tepid and there weren't any rocks to fall. The little occasional blinks of lightning were weak. There weren't any wild things to run for cover.

She leaned her elbows on the counter and stared down through the glass at the rings and watches there. She wondered what it would be like to own a wristwatch. Or a diamond ring.

After a while Mr. Zabowski came out and said she could

go home. He looked sick and admitted that he was. He said he was going to close shop for the day.

She walked home through the lessening rain.

Her father and the children had had a visitor named Elijah. Elijah had a biscuit-colored beard and large, luminous eyes the color of ripe blackberries. Elijah had sold the Proffitts a potato skinner for one dollar and a pair of chinchillas for eight. Elijah would deliver the chinchillas that night along with a cage. Elijah then would explain how to make money with these animals. They bred like rabbits. In just no time at all the Proffitts would be in a big, money-making business of their own. The little kids would share their room with the money-makers. The two beds could be pushed close together to make room for all the cages they'd need. Chinchillas didn't eat much and didn't stink. Elijah had shown them pictures of the beautiful, furred creatures. Furriers paid enormous sums of money for them. Furriers were people who made fur coats for people. There were lots of these down in the Loop and they needed chinchilla skins bad. Rich women were crazy about chinchilla coats and if they couldn't get a full coat they'd settle for a muff or a little hat. On the other side of Chicago there was a slew of rich women, all just dying for anything made out of chinchilla.

Trailed by the excited, chattering little kids, Marvella came out of their bedroom and looked at her father sitting in his chair. There was an assertiveness in the lift of his chin that she hadn't seen for a long time. He was skinning the supper potatoes with the tool Elijah had sold him. "Elijah'll be back with the chinchillas 'long about dark," he said. "We should eat early."

"Where's Zollie?" Marvella asked.

The little kids shook their heads. "We don't know. She didn't come home yet. Juanita didn't either."

Marvella took the pan of potatoes from her father's lap and carried them to the kitchen. Hugh and Arlie followed her. "It'll be good Pa can be busy again," said Hugh.

"It's something all of us can work at," said Arlie. "Even me. Elijah said so. I really like him."

"He's a gent," observed Hugh.

Marvella sliced the potatoes and set them on the stove to fry. Arlie, without being told, went to the bathroom, washed his hands, and came back to set the table for the evening meal. Presently they sat down to eat though Zollie and Juanita still had not come and now the under-dusk was beginning to color the alley and the buildings, and the sky above them, clean from the rain, began to exchange its day colors for night ones.

"Wouldn't it be funny," said Dwain, the pessimistic one, "if Zollie had just taken up and left us? Her and Juanita?"

The other little kids screamed their disbelieving laughter. "Zollie ain't ever a-going to leave us! She loves us! She says so all the time! You crazy, Dwain?"

"She'll be home directly," said Dorman Proffitt. "More'n likely her and Juanita are having to work late. Is it dark yet?"

The little kids moved with the father into the front room and sat down to wait for Elijah to come with the money-making chinchillas. They waited for Zollie and Juanita. As the night advanced they waited more and more anxiously. On the stairway outside their door things scuttled and squeaked and they investigated each sound. They stood at the window and looked down into the alley and soon they understood about Elijah and spoke of him bitterly.

"Prob'ly," said Hugh, "his name wasn't even Elijah. I thought there might be something funny about him when he was doing all that big talking but I didn't want to say anything."

"He's a thief," declared Dwain. "That's all. He took our eight dollars and we didn't get anything for it."

"We should find out where he lives," said Noah. "And go to his house and beat him up."

"Maybe he just forgot," said Arlie. "But I don't think so. He's a thief, that's all, and now our eight dollars is gone."

Ashamed and dejected, their father sat kneading his bony knees. "It was a mistake," he said. "We didn't know. We just didn't know."

Standing at the window Marvella thought she saw Zollie and Juanita coming. She pulled the curtain back to get a better look and her father, sensing this interest, asked, "Is Zollie coming?"

The two figures at the far end of the alley turned into a doorway and disappeared. Marvella let the curtain drop back into place. "No, Pa."

Dwain stared hard at her. He was the first to voice his fear. "What if something's happened to her? What if a car's run over her or something like that?"

Inexpertly Noah hid behind brave words. "It couldn't have. We'd have known about it if it had. Somebody would've come and told us."

"Who?" asked Dwain with deep meaning. "Who? And how would they know to come here? It's not like Goose Elk, don't forget. Where everybody knows everybody else. There are so many here just one missing don't make a smidgen of difference. So if Zollie's got herself run over or something like that who's going to notice and come tell us?"

Arlie started to cry and Hugh turned on him. "What're you bawling about? There's nothing to bawl about. You should know Dwain by now; you should know how he likes to scare people. Nothing's happened to Zollie. She'll be here in a minute."

"She won't be," wailed Arlie. "A car's run over her and nobody's going to come tell us. They don't know we're here."

"Oh, faugh," said Hugh and Arlie's grief rose to a shrill, frustrated pitch.

In his corner their father said something but amid the clamor his words were lost. Marvella glanced at him and turned to her brothers, taking charge of the situation. "Hush. All of you hush. Go wash for bed. Nothing's happened to Zollie. She'll be home any minute now. Go wash and go to bed and no back talk either."

The little kids went, pushing and jostling each other, wrestling at the door to the bathroom to see who would go in first. Hugh won and went in but returned in a minute for Arlie and Arlie kicked him.

In the kitchen Marvella washed and dried the dishes and made numerous trips to the window to look down into the alley. Now the night had softened its countenance; the row of garbage cans and the Proffitts' old car and the stained mattress were just barely discernible in the maze of darkness. Above the alley there was a sliver of moon and white stars winked. Across the way Mrs. Haliki's dim light burned. Marvella could see the old woman moving back and forth setting up an ironing board to press a garment, going to the table to nibble and drink. Her occupations seemed cheerless and after a moment Marvella turned away from the window. She left the kitchen and went to the front room where her father had fallen asleep in his chair.

The little kids were asleep, too, all except Hugh. Hugh was wide awake. "Has Zollie come yet?" he whispered.

Marvella took Arlie's thumb from his mouth. "No."

Hugh sat up. "Something's happened to her, Marvella. I just know it. She wouldn't stay gone this long without telling us. Something's happened to her. We should go and find out."

Marvella looked at him. To be fourteen and not to be wise, she thought. It's awful. The prospect of something happening to Zollie was dismal and terrifying. She said, "Well, I don't know. I don't know where to start. Where do you think we should start?"

Hugh got out of bed and started putting his clothes on over his pajamas. He was worrying his lower lip with his teeth. "We'll go ask Frank. Frank'll know. Have you got a flashlight? We'll need one or some matches, I think."

The sliver of moon above the alley had moved out to the open sky and now a fresh breeze coursed the length of the cement aisle. Among the garbage cans curious, hungry scavengers, intent on their own desperate pursuits, clawed their way through the dank piles of the sluttish stuff there and their squeaks of discovery were muffled. Marvella and Hugh did not hear them as they went past the cans and entered the building where Frank lived.

"This way," said Hugh and they went up the stairs and down the dark corridor to Frank's door and Marvella knocked on it.

Frank said they should go to the nearest police station. "They're a bunch of clunkheads down there but it's the only thing to do this time of night. Wait a second. I'd better go with you. This ain't a job for no hillbillies. Just wait a second in the corner over there, huh? I'd ask you to sit down but as you can see we've only got one chair and my mother here is using it. She's weak from having worked hard all day. Else I'd ask her to get up and let you have it."

Frank's mother who was reading a magazine didn't look up. "Faugh," she said.

"That's the only word she knows," said Frank and laughed. He was in a high mood. He made jokes all the way to the police station. Marvella and Hugh did not respond. They walked close to each other and looked straight ahead.

By night the city looked different than it did by day. It was glossier. To Marvella it seemed a place that had run amuck with its gloss; the gaudy signs on the buildings and above them flashing red, orange, green, and purple. Over these, distant and unimportant, the sliver of moon and the white stars seemed unnatural. The people, pushing and being pushed, seemed unnatural, too. At a bus stop Marvella saw a man viciously elbow his way to the front of the curb so as to be first to board an approaching bus. The other people grouped there cursed him and jabbed him with their own elbows but the man only smiled and stood his ground. I hate him, thought Marvella, surprising herself with the passionate intensity of this thought. Hugh had reached for her hand and she gripped it in her own.

At the police station the three from the alley stood in front of a desk and stated their mission. "It's our step-mother," said Marvella. "She didn't come home today. She's been gone since six o'clock this morning."

With a practiced twist the man behind the desk inserted a sheet of paper in his typewriter. "What's her name?"

"Mrs. Zollie Proffitt."

The man typed. "Address?"

Frank supplied the address.

The man wanted a description of Zollie and Marvella and Hugh furnished it. The man wanted the name of the hotel where Zollie worked and the two Proffitts looked at each other blankly. "We don't know," they confessed. "She said it was a big one."

The man controlled his sigh.

"Do you think you can find her?" asked Marvella. "My aunt was with her when she left this morning to go to work. I just don't see how two grown-up people can disappear like this, do you? What will you do? Where will you look?"

The man had risen but now he sat back down again. He took a fresh piece of paper from a drawer to write Juanita's name and description on. He was annoyed.

Frank had stepped up close to the desk. He flung his hair back. "We want to know what you're going to do. How you're going to find these two people if it ain't asking too much."

The man was clipping the two papers—the one with Juanita's description and the one with Zollie's—together. "We'll find them. Don't worry."

Frank was looking hard at the policeman. "My two friends here don't know about stuff like this. Why don't you tell them how you're gonna find their aunt and stepmother so they can go home and go to sleep?"

The policeman sighed. With the two pieces of paper in his hand he stood and looked down at the three from the alley. Something old and wary and tired flickered once across his rough face. "We'll find them," he said. "Don't worry, we'll find them. As soon as we have we'll come and tell you. Go home and go to sleep now." With the papers in his hand he turned and went toward an inner door and disappeared through it and after a moment Hugh and Marvella and Frank went back out to the street and walked home.

꧁

CHAPTER SIX

꧁

The police did not find Zollie and Juanita. The two had simply vanished and now for those left in the pink apartment above the alley there came a time harder than any they had ever experienced.

The very first thing to be faced was how they were to live. "We'll live," said Dorman Proffitt. "We always have. That's one thing Zollie's running off and leaving us ain't going to change. We'll live."

Gathered around their father, looking to him for the comfort he could not give, waiting to hear him speak the words of salvation he could not speak, the little kids and Marvella avoided looking at each other. The fear in the room was a living quality. Zollie and Juanita were both gone; now their absence had stretched close to fifty hours. They weren't coming back not even for their clothes or to say good-bye. Nothing terrible had happened to them; all the dead bodies from accidents and murders had been brought to the city's morgues and identified and none had been Juanita or Zollie. They were just gone. It happened. It wasn't anything new, not to the police. They had seen it happen hundreds of times. Probably Zollie and Juanita had been plotting it all along, for months maybe. There was never any telling what was in other people's minds.

At first the little kids had cried; even Hugh had spent an uncomfortable time with himself in the bathroom. That was over though now. Now they had to think and act. If only this could have happened back in Goose Elk, Hugh thought. If it had happened then we could have gone to the Critchers and said looka here, we need some help. And the Critchers would have given it. They poisoned our hogs and run us out of the valley; they're particular mean, all right, but they would have helped us. Here there's nobody, not even anybody to ask what to do. Pa doesn't know. He's blind. He can't even find his bed by hisself.

Marvella was saying, "Pa's right. We'll live. I'm working and that's something. Mr. Zabowski hasn't paid me yet but tomorrow I'll ask him to and then we'll know better how to plan things. We shouldn't be worrying ourselves like this. There's nothing to worry about. We got along all right before Zollie came; we'll get along all right now, too."

Hugh stirred. Ashamed by his father's helplessness and his own fear, he spoke sharply. "I'll get a job. I'll ask Frank where to look for one. He'll know."

"We'll all get jobs!" cried Noah. "We don't need Zollie! We can get along by ourselves!"

"We'll do it tomorrow," declared Dwain. "Not today because it's Sunday. Tomorrow though. We'll show Zollie. We'll show her we don't need her."

"I don't like her any more," said Arlie tremulously. "When she comes back I'm going to tell her that."

"We'll make out," said Dorman Proffitt and sat up straighter in his chair, showing his children that his knowledge of the world had not completely faded. The children smiled at their father. Now they were united—all of them together in this hard, unexpected thing—and there was strength and a certain kind of happiness in this.

"I'd better go find Frank," said Hugh. "And talk to him."

"Tell him we *all* want jobs!" shouted Noah. "Not just you! All of us!" He ran ahead of Hugh to the door, stumbling over his own feet in his excitement.

Hugh and the other little kids followed. They went down the stairs and into the alley. Somewhere a church bell was ringing. The calm beauty of its slow, measured tones floated down across the tops of the buildings.

Frank and Mario were sitting on the mattress. A watermelon which had been cut in half lay on a piece of brown butcher's paper between them. Taking turns with Frank's knife they were cutting big chunks from the melon's insides, stuffing the frosty, pink meat into their mouths, letting the juice run down their chins, rolling their eyes in enjoyment. They didn't offer the Proffitt boys any. "It was a present from me to Mario," said Frank. "He needs stuff like this to eat. The doctor said so. You can have half of the next one. I'll go after it pretty soon."

Hugh and his brothers sat down on the far end of the mattress, away from the watermelon.

Hugh studied his fingernails. In disgust he saw that the ones on his right hand were bitten clean down to the flesh. Nail biting was a habit he had broken himself of a long time ago but now apparently it was back to be dealt with again. He shoved his hand in his pocket. He looked at Frank. "Frank, I got to talk to you."

65

"It's about jobs," said Noah eagerly. "We've all got to get one now. Zollie's not coming back to take care of us any more so now we've got to take care of ourselves. We've all got to get jobs. Where should we go to look for 'em, Frank?"

Frank spat watermelon seeds. Without any hesitation he said, "There ain't any jobs here. For grown-ups maybe there are some but not any for kids."

"Back home," said Dwain. "Back home we worked. In the fields. We worked hard. Last summer and summer before Mr. Critcher gave us all jobs. We planted potatoes, whole acres of them—"

"And hoed strawberries," supplied Noah.

"Yes. We did that. And helped Mr. Critcher with his bees and his chickens. We worked hard and he paid us. Not enough, Zollie said, but he paid us. We worked. That's what we want to do here. We want work."

With his knife Frank carved another hunk of the watermelon and handed it to Mario. "There ain't any work like that around here. It's just all stores and business. And nobody wants to hire kids. We make trouble, they say. We break things and steal. I had a job one time. It didn't last long though. It was in a bakery."

Watching Mario slurping the cold, sweet melon chunks, Hugh's mind harkened back to the time he and the other little kids had last had a watermelon. It hadn't been so long ago. It had been in June when Arlie's birthday came. They had had a watermelon and Zollie had baked a white cake. They had all sung happy birthday to Arlie and given him presents. Had it only been in June? Now Zollie was gone; she wasn't coming back even to tell them good-bye and now, from somewhere, they had to have money. Hugh turned his head to look directly at Frank. "This job you had in the bakery. How did you find it?"

Frank flung his long, black hair back. "My old lady got it for me."

"You mean your mother?"

Mario wetly laughed.

"I washed pans in that place till my arms almost dropped off," said Frank. "I never did get done. The day they took me away to get corrected the pans was stacked in the sinks to the ceiling."

"Corrected from what?" asked Hugh.

Frank's smile was slow and gravely gentle. "From stealing. One morning the old lady that run this place went out for a minute and I went to the front and took two dollars from the cash register. She said I took twenty but it was only two. They sent me away to a place to get corrected. It wasn't so bad; I didn't mind it. I wish I was there now."

Hugh twisted the hand in his pocket into a fist. "About us getting jobs, Frank."

"There ain't any," said Frank. " 'Course you could try but you'd just be wasting your time. Instead your dad or your sister should see about getting you some free money."

"What's free money?"

Gently Frank studied him. "You hillbillies. You don't know anything, do you? Free money is money you get from the Government. You go down to their office and tell them you're starving to death and can't find a job and then they send somebody out to see if you're telling the truth. Then when they find out you are, they start sending you free money."

The other little kids had drawn closer to Hugh and Frank. Their eyes were shining. "We didn't know anything about this—"

"Why didn't you tell us before?"

"Free money? We don't have any of *that* in Goose Elk—"

"We'd better go tell Pa and Marvella!"

The little kids, all but Hugh, scrambled to their feet and raced away across the alley, toward the stairs to their building.

For a long moment Frank and Mario and Hugh were silent. Mario had finished with the watermelon. He rolled the glutted halves of it in the butcher's paper and carried the bundle over to the garbage cans.

Frank stretched his legs but remained seated on the mattress. "I should've told you it takes an awful long time to get started with the government people," he said. "An awful long time. Months. First they got to come and look you over. They even look in your cupboards. They write everything down. All your names, how old you are, what color you are, if you own any valuables, everything. Then they go back to their office and talk that over. Then they come back and ask some more questions. It takes an awful long time. Months. And even after the money starts coming they keep coming back treating you like liars and criminals. I don't like it but that's how we live. Mario and his mother, too. It ain't much; there's never any left over for extras. Any extras, you got to find ways to get 'em yourself."

Something inside Hugh made an uneasy movement. Frank's expression was simple and pleasant but there was something odd and secret in it, too. He met Frank's eyes. "Did you go where you said you were going to? Did you go to the Loop yet? Is that where the watermelon came from?"

Frank took some green money-bills and some silver from his pocket. He spread it out on the mattress and began to count it. He might have been counting matchsticks so casual and offhand he was. But now in his dark eyes and the set of his soft mouth there was a fierce pride. "I went to the Loop and I came back with this. More than this. Some of it I spent already. For the watermelon and Mario and me went to the movies last night. Tomorrow we're going to take Mario to a paid doctor; there might not be enough here for that. I don't know."

The church bells had stopped ringing. The Sunday stillness in the alley was very warm. Hugh put his left hand to his mouth and began to bite his nails. He wanted to hear and yet didn't want to hear about Frank's trip to the Loop. It must've been a pretty scary thing—pretty dangerous. It took a lot of . . . of something to do a thing like that. To run up to some-body who was just walking along and snatch their purse.

Frank was folding the bills, tucking them back into his pocket and gathering up the change. He was saying, "I never pick a real poor one. I look at their clothes first. You tell peo-ple by their clothes a lot. If their clothes ain't good I let it go. If they're good I go ahead with it."

Anxiety rose in Hugh. "I don't think you can tell people by their clothes so much. Back home in Goose Elk Mr. Simpson —he owns the general store and has got plenty of money— he wears overalls. I don't think you can tell people by their clothes. Some people get dressed up just to go places. To town and church and stuff. So if you pick people just by their clothes . . . well, sometimes you might get a wrong one. Then what?"

"I don't think about it."

"Not ever? Not even when you're by yourself?"

Frank flung his hair back and looked across to the row of garbage cans where Mario was still standing. Mrs. Haliki had come to her window to look out at Mario. He was leaning, lifting a stack of newspaper, to peer at what was beneath. "I don't think about it," repeated Frank. "I just do what I think is right at the time and if it's wrong, well, I can't help it." He slid his hand down over his dirty shirt and pants. With a grimace of distaste he eyed his feet; at one time the sneakers on them had been white but now with broken laces and flapping soles they were unbelievably filthy. "I hate being dirty all the time," he said. "Tomorrow Mario and me are going to go to one of those steam places and have ourselves a good bath. Hot, with lots of soap."

"Tomorrow I'm going to get a job," said Hugh.

The church bells were ringing again, filling the alley with their long, solemn peals.

Hugh had been to a dozen places or more in search of a job but now on this Monday, at high noon, he had to admit to himself that Frank had been right. There just weren't any jobs—not for kids. The people he had applied to had laughed at him, jeered at him, ignored him, been sarcastic and amused and mean. They had caused twinges in his stomach. They had scared him and angered him. They had lowered his pride to a depth he hadn't known was possible. He had been surly after that happened and had shuffled from store to store and from shop to shop in an ever-increasing sour awareness of self: He was an outsider, a hillbilly who spoke and acted like one. The old Goose Elk standards didn't work here. Nor the Golden Rule. They had viewed his friendliness and politeness with suspicion. They had been suspicious of him, a hillbilly from Goose Elk, North Carolina. One old man had cursed him. There hadn't been any call for that at all; he hadn't *meant* to push those eggs off that counter. It had just happened. Probably they had been rotten anyway, they had sure smelled like they were. But the old man had cursed him and ordered him out. There wasn't any call for these people being the way they were. He might be a hillbilly but these people were worse. They were like . . . like wild dogs. Pushing and grabbing and snarling. They were terrible.

Bitterly sick of the whole thing, Hugh now approached Zabowski's store. Marvella was standing in the doorway of it flapping a rag. She beckoned to him and he went over to her. "Did you find anything?" she asked.

"No. I been everywhere, too. All up and down all these streets. Nobody wants to hire a little kid. They just laughed at me."

Marvella said, "Oh. Oh, Hugh."

"I looked, I tell ya! I looked everywhere! I asked everybody! These people are crazy! They laugh at things that aren't funny and half of them don't know how to speak English and they blame it on you 'cause you don't know their talk and . . . and they're crazy!"

Marvella's lips had gone tight. She glanced over her shoulder to the dim interior of the store then stepped outside on the street. She took Hugh's hand and pulled him along several steps until they stood under Zabowski's window sign. "I asked about my pay this morning," she said, speaking solemnly and urgently. "Hugh, it's only ten dollars a week."

He stared at her. "Ten dollars a week! But . . . but that's just nothing! Last night when we wrote it all down and figured out how much we had to have . . . Ten dollars!"

"Mr. Zabowski won't give me any more, Hugh. I told him I'd work longer every day and he said no. That's all he can pay me."

Troubled and hot, Hugh considered. "The government people then. They'll have to help us. Did you go to their office yet?"

"I went about an hour ago. Mr. Zabowski let me off to do it."

"What'd they say?"

"They'll come but it'll take a while. It won't be today or tomorrow. They're shorthanded, the lady said. They don't have enough people to go around. It might be a week or two before she can send somebody. She wasn't very nice."

Just like Frank said, thought Hugh. Everything's just like he said. First no job and now this. It'll take months. When they do come they'll treat us like liars and criminals. Frank's right about a lot of things. He's smarter'n I am. He can think like a grown-up. That danged Zollie, running off and leaving us in a fix like this. To come all this way just to earn ten dollars. We could have done this good back in Goose Elk where everything was practically free. That danged Zollie. I hope she's dead.

Marvella was saying, "I thought we could sell the car. It's no good to us now that Zollie's gone. Pa can't drive it and I'm afraid to. It'd be a lot different than driving around in the fields back home. So why don't we sell it? I think we could get enough for it to keep us going until the government money starts coming."

Tired and now thoroughly depressed, Hugh sighed. "All right. I'll ask Frank."

"It's the only way, Hugh. We're stuck."

"I'll go find Frank now," said Hugh and moved away from her and started off down the street at a trot. He went past a little boy who was being pulled along by his mother. The child was placidly licking an ice cream cone; he grinned at Hugh but Hugh did not grin back.

Mothers and ice cream cones were both a part of a lost, brighter childhood. Neither had anything to do with him any more.

Through Frank's ingenuity there came a man to the alley, a possible buyer for the Proffitts' car. He walked around it, kicking the deflated tires. The missing hubcaps saddened him. He looked at what was beneath the hood and hissed through his teeth. He asked for the ignition key and Hugh handed it to him.

The car wouldn't start. "Because it's just been setting here so long," said Hugh. "It runs good. It's a good car, mister. How much'll you give us for it?"

The man got out of the car and walked around it again. He kicked the flattened tires and hissed. "Seventy-five dollars. You can go up and tell your daddy I'll give him seventy-five dollars for it." Frank, who was standing nearby watching, flung his hair back and lifted his eyes to heaven. He spoke with knowledgeable contempt. "Seventy-five dollars. You'll get twice that for it on your lot. I know youse guys. I lived here all my life. I ain't no hillbilly like these others here."

The man ignored Frank. He looked at Hugh. "I ain't got all day, sonny."

Dorman Proffitt would have sold the car that day to this person but there was the matter of the title. This document, taken from Dorman Proffitt's wallet, stated that the car legally belonged to Zollie. It couldn't be sold without her signature.

"But she ain't here," protested Hugh. "She's gone and

nobody knows where. Besides the car ain't hers. It's Pa's."

"I only," informed Dorman Proffitt gently, "put it in her name because of my eyes."

The car man had risen. "Well, I can't buy it without the title."

There wasn't any help for this. Even Frank couldn't think of a workable remedy.

Hugh and Frank were walking along a busy, downtown street. It was night and the great, neon lamps of Chicago had been lit. Some of them were steadfast and some blinked on and off. They were bright and splendid, all colors and all sizes and shapes, an achievement that hadn't been done by halves, this man-made constellation. No one was paying any attention to the lights. The people were hurrying to theaters, were loitering before store windows, were standing on the street corners idly watching other people.

Frank and Hugh moved across the wide, windy avenue and stood in a shadowed doorway. The erratic beat of Hugh's heart—first slow thuds and then rapid knocks—was stifling him. He had his clenched fists in his pockets; his gnawed nails were painful against his palms.

Frank was saying, "You got to watch the street, stupid. You can't just stand there with your eyes closed. We didn't come here to sleep. You're not scared, are you?"

Hugh opened his eyes and focused them on Frank. " 'Course I'm scared. I don't like it. I never done anything like this before. I feel sick. I don't think we should go through with it. I think we should forget it and go home."

"The first time is always the worst," said Frank sympathetically. "After that it gets easier. You got it straight in your mind what to do now, huh?"

74

"Yes."

"What? Go over it again."

Hugh licked his lips. "First watch for one that's dressed good. She shouldn't have anybody with her. She should just be walking along by herself. Nobody around. She should be carrying her purse by the handle or under her arm. I shouldn't run at her. I should just step out and kind of walk along with her. When we reach . . . reach the corner I should grab the purse away from her and run in the other direction. As I'm running I should take all the money out—her billfold and change purse."

"Feel for jewelry," prompted Frank. "Sometimes women carry jewelry in their purses."

"Yes. And then . . . then I should throw it somewhere. In a trash can or doorway or something."

"Then you should stop running—"

"Yes. Then I should stop running—"

"Walk natural—"

"Walk natural. Yes."

"Go to the nearest bus stop."

"Yes. Go to the nearest bus stop."

"Get on the bus."

"Get on the bus. Yes."

"Ride a coupla blocks. Get off. Take another bus—the right one—and go home. I'll get through before you do; I'll meet you there. I'll be waiting for youse."

Hugh looked at Frank and a vivid picture of what was at home came sliding into his mind. Pa would be sitting in his chair in the corner dreaming of bygone things. Of the farm in Goose Elk and when he had been boss of it. Lately Pa was a little on the foolish side. The fix they were in hadn't seemed to sink in on him. All he did was dream of things past and talk about things that weren't real. The mimosa tree growing in the alley, for instance. He asked about the tree every night and wanted it described to him. Which was all right. Everybody dreamed at some time or another. But right now was a mighty ill-convenient time for it. For dreaming about trees that weren't there and government people coming with handfuls of free money. For supper there had been fried cornmeal mush and not much else. Marvella had dished it up without any excuses. What was the use in asking excuses for something you couldn't help? Because he was so little and didn't know the fix they were in, Arlie had asked for milk and loudly complained when Marvella had only poured him a small glass. Arlie was a pest. Of course it wasn't his fault that he was a baby. Still wouldn't you think he'd sense something was wrong and not holler for things? The other little kids didn't. Arlie was the only one. Somebody should tell him . . . tell him how things were.

Thinking about Arlie and the other little kids and Marvella and Pa and the fix they were in somehow strengthened Hugh. If there was to be any relief from things it would be him that would have to bring it about. So no use to just stand here dreading what had to be done.

Hugh spoke to his friend. "All right. I've got it all fixed in my mind. I'll get it done. You go on now to your own work. I'll be home in just a little bit. Wait for me near the mattress."

Frank left him and Hugh began to critically appraise the people that passed his doorway. Now the desire to get through with this and not to bungle it in the doing was the only important thing. Frank would laugh at him if he bungled and other, worse things would happen, too. So much depended.

A light, misty rain had begun to fall and the wind, coming in from someplace that was fresh and moist, swept along the avenue. Across the street there was a brightly lighted restaurant and people were going into it and coming out of it. The delicious smell of roasted meat reached Hugh's nostrils. With his sleeve he wiped moisture from his face and waited and watched. Not too many people on this side of the street; for some reason they all preferred the other.

But there. A woman coming toward him. Alone. A purse with a long handle swinging from her hand. Dressed good. She came abreast of him and went past. She didn't look in his direction. He stepped out and fell into step behind her. She didn't look around. He quickened his pace and still she didn't look around. The rain had thickened; it felt cold on his face.

The woman ahead of him had slowed, she was pausing to look in a store window. Something in Hugh's ears desperately throbbed. It was only a few steps to the corner. Then around it and away. He could do it. There was no one to stop him. Even if she screamed it would take the people on the other side too long. On this side there was only himself and the woman.

Now. Hugh darted to the woman and snatched the purse from her hand. She whirled and all in an instant Hugh saw her open mouth and shocked eyes and her stiff, gray-white hair shining in front from the rain. Her mouth was a black hole. She didn't scream.

He was around the corner and was running. He had the purse open and was transferring what was in it to his pockets. He was remembering to search the inner folds of the purse for jewelry.

CHAPTER SEVEN

The rain had ceased but had left in its wake in the alley dark, lustrous puddles that steamed. Light, faintly streaming from some of the windows along the thoroughfare, illuminated the puddles and cast long, mystic shadows on the damp cement.

Crouched on the mattress with the night's take spread out between them, Hugh and Frank were holding a business conference, hashing over the details of the past two hours. Now that the thing was done Hugh found himself feeling a certain pride. He hadn't bungled it. It had all come off as smoothly as clockwork. Oh, he had been scared at first; when Frank had left him and then, at the moment of its actual happening and the woman had looked at him—that part had been bad. She shouldn't have looked at him. But now it was over. He could forget the woman. He would never see her again. Even if someday, when he was grown, and wanted to find her and explain, he wouldn't be able to. There were too many in this city; if he looked for a hundred years he'd never be able to find her. After a while the unease in him would go away. It would. Already, persuaded by a logic he hadn't known was in him, it was flowing away from him. The woman shouldn't have been there alone; she should have had a man with her. She shouldn't have been carrying her purse that way, swinging it from her hand. She shouldn't have had that much money in her purse; if she had had less she wouldn't miss it so much.

Frank was counting the bills again, touching and spreading and smoothing them lovingly. He was saying, "Eighty-six dollars. Not so bad for a firster."

Awed and almost overcome with excitement Hugh shifted his weight from one haunch to the other. "I did it all just like we said. When I saw her coming toward me I waited. I didn't run out at her. Then when she got a little past me I went out and walked along in back of her. Quiet. She didn't hear me. There were a lot of people on the other side of the street but just me and her on ours. She stopped and looked in a window and I went up behind her."

Frank had tired of the account. He had heard it twice. He had picked up one of the bills—a ten—and was wrapping it around his thumb. "You were lucky. I only got four dollars and I almost killed myself getting away. She screamed her head off."

"Mine didn't scream," said Hugh. "She just stood there. It was the funniest thing."

Frank took the ten-dollar bill from his thumb. Being casual and friendly, he said, "You owe me this so I'll just take it now. Actually what I charge guys is ten percent so by rights I should give you back a dollar forty. But I won't in this

79

case. You owe me bus fare and I spent more time on this case than I usually do. I want you to lend me another ten."

"For what?"

Frank laughed. "Already you're greedy. I never seen it fail when a guy gets a few dollars. You'd think it was God. I have to take Mario to the doctor tomorrow. Come on; you can afford it. Hand it over. I'll pay you interest on it if you want."

"Interest?"

"Hillbilly."

"Well, what's interest?"

"Interest," explained Frank, "is what rich guys charge poor ones for the use of their money. You mean you don't know about interest?"

"No. Here's your ten bill. Don't forget I want it back."

"You want me to pay you interest?"

"I guess so."

"How much?"

Hugh considered. He had never been much good at figures but this interest . . . well, it might be worthwhile. Besides he hadn't reckoned on paying Frank any commission. That part hadn't been mentioned. It was fair enough—it just hadn't been mentioned. It was kind of sneaky come to think of it. After a minute Hugh said, "I guess twenty percent would be all right."

The pink apartment was dim and silent. Everyone was asleep. Hugh stood in the dark kitchen and drank three glasses of water and after that had coldly settled went to Marvella's room and woke her. He switched on the light and showed her the money. She sat up and stared at him. "Where did you get it?"

"I got it," he answered. "Don't ask questions. Just take it."

"Hugh—"

"Don't ask questions, I tell ya! Just put it somewheres until tomorrow. Tomorrow we'll buy food. Maybe we could have some meat. And get Arlie some milk; a gallon of it."

Marvella got out of bed. She took the money and went to the dresser and opened a drawer. In just her cotton slip she was too skinny. The sight of her skinny arms and legs twinged Hugh's stomach. He was tired and now the earlier elation had gone. Frank could say all he wanted about how easy it was to steal money but it wasn't easy. It was work. There was danger in it and afterward . . . afterward you didn't feel so good. The thoughts came—bad ones—and once they started there wasn't any way you could shut them off.

From Marvella's face Hugh could tell that they weren't going to talk about the money. Marvella was putting on her dress. She was holding herself careful, away from things. She was saying, "Yes, we'll have meat and milk. I'll be careful though, when I buy. We'll have to make what we have stretch till the government money starts coming. There's some cocoa. I could make us a hot drink. Would you like that?"

They sat in the kitchen and drank their hot, water-cocoa drink. Beneath their window there came a scuffling noise and they got up to look down. Two men were fighting in the alley, running at each other, cursing, reeling, pummeling. They fell and rose and staggered away from each other to look for weapons. One of them emptied a garbage can and raised it high and hurled it. The other broke the neck from a bottle and with this in hand went charging. There was a long, agonized scream and then silence.

"One of them's killed the other," whispered Hugh. "Look,

he's running away. Do you think we should go down? Call the police maybe?"

Others from across the alley had heard the fight. Lights had come on and doorways had cracked. But no one had come out. The figure of the dead or injured one lay motionless, something near his twisted head glistening.

No one came out to see about him. Presently the doors across the way were closed again and the lights went out, one by one.

"Awful," whispered Hugh. "It's just awful. If this was in Goose Elk we'd go down to see about him. Why don't we? Why don't the others? They've lived here longer and they're grown-ups."

"I think they might be afraid," whispered Marvella. "I am, too. Come away. Don't look any more. It isn't . . . it isn't for us."

In the morning the man was gone. Mrs. Haliki came out with a bucket of sudsy water and washed away the signs the fight had left. There was a trail of them.

Mario put up a good-natured fight against going to the doctor. Frank and Hugh had to force him from his bed and stand him on his feet and put his clothes on him. All the time they were doing this he pretended to be a rag doll. He made his body go limp and flopped his legs and arms and slid to the floor the instant either of the other two boys let go of him. When Frank mentioned that Mario should put on shoes and socks Mario screamed with laughter. "That doctor ain't going to look at my feet! Whatsa matter with you? I told him a thousand times I don't walk straight sometimes but he ain't looked yet."

"Shut up," ordered Frank. "This time we're taking you to a different doctor. Put your shoes and socks on and comb your hair."

Mario sat on the edge of his rumpled bed and put his shoes and socks on. "We got an appointment to see this doctor?"

"Yes," answered Frank.

Mario giggled. " 'Twon't do no good. You know what he'll say? He'll say I've got epilepsy which I already know. He'll say I should go to the country and live and take medicine every day and eat good. He'll say where is my mother and I'll say asleep. She sleeps all the time. She's asleep now."

"Hurry it up," said Frank. "We're going to be late for our appointment. Comb your hair."

Mario stood up and capered toward the mirror. He picked up a comb and surveyed the grimy dresser top, empty save for a small tray of pins and loose matches. "There's no goop for it," he complained. "I can't go to no doctor with my hair standing out like this. Look at it. Every time the comb comes near it, it jumps. That steam bath you forced me into the other day might've purified my pores but look what it done to my hair."

Frank went to the kitchen and came back with a blob of white lard in his hand. He dropped it on the crown of Mario's head and with his palms Mario started working it into his hair. Soon the strands of it, black and oiled, were obedient.

The three boys left the apartment and went down the stairs and outside to the alley. The smaller Proffitt children were down at the far end of it listlessly playing catch-ball. Dwain called out to Hugh, "Hey, where're you going?"

Arlie came running up to him. "Marvella's gone to buy groceries. She doesn't have to work today because . . . she went and then came back. Now she's gone for groceries. Where are you going? Can I go with you?"

Hugh looked at Frank. "Lend me a dollar of my interest money."

Frank took a dollar from his pocket and handed it to Hugh. Hugh pressed the money into his brother's hand. "For ice cream. But not now. After a while. Tell Dwain I said to go after it. And remember to take Pa some. Tell Marvella I've gone with Frank and Mario. I'll be back in a little bit."

Clutching the precious dollar Arlie trotted off and Hugh and Frank and Mario walked to the exit of the alley and went out to the street.

Hugh felt good. The fear and unease of the night before had already been absorbed by some mysterious process that worked for his benefit. What had happened in the Loop and then later on, the two men fighting in the alley—those things were still in his mind—prob'ly forever they would stay there. Prob'ly at times they would plague him, especially the memory of the woman standing in the rain with her shocked mouth open and her shocked eyes looking down at him. But not now. Now, because of some power he had, he was able to dwell on them in semi-peaceful conscience. Or not dwell on them at all, whichever way his fancy chose. Now he felt good. He had provided for his family and that made him the head of things—the one in charge. He wouldn't ever again be just one of "the little kids." That had happened to him, too—overnight. In some way not yet completely understood he was older and wiser and stronger. Let the little kids have their ice cream; he was glad he had been able to get it for them. He had more important things to do than sit around licking ice cream cones. He was on his way to help his friends. Maybe the doctor would ask *him* how Mario had acted during his last fit. He'd be able to say. Prob'ly better than Frank he'd be able to say because he had watched it closer than Frank. Frank had been too busy to actually watch. Funny. Mario didn't look sick. What was epilepsy? He'd ask Marvella.

Stepping along down the avenue with his friends, Hugh breathed deeply and felt good. For supper tonight there would be meat; maybe a beef roast with brown gravy and potatoes.

Hugh and Frank and Mario sat in the doctor's office looking at magazines. The appointment had been for nine o'clock but now it was almost eleven and still the doctor hadn't come. He was at the hospital the nurse had said. He had been detained unexpectedly. She was sorry for the delay. The doctor was terribly busy; so many patients depending on him. They should just sit quietly and read the magazines. They shouldn't bother her every five minutes. She was busy, too. They should just sit quietly and read the magazines.

Mario didn't like his magazine. Impatiently he kept flicking the slick pages of it back and forth. "If this doctor's so busy he don't even know what time it is we should just get up and go. Our appointment was for nine o'clock; now it's eleven."

The waiting room was filled with people, some of them obviously pretty sick, and Frank was respecting them. He kept his voice low. "Be quiet. We're here now and we're just gonna have to wait our turn. Read your magazine."

Mario made small popping sounds with his mouth. He crossed and uncrossed his legs. He pleated his shirt tail. He sighed loudly. "If everybody in this room just got up and left then the doctor wouldn't be busy no more, would he?"

"Be quiet," said Frank.

85

"Poor fella," droned Mario. "I feel sorry for him. All these people depending on him. He's only got one head and one set of legs and two hands. Unless he's deformed, that is. People should think about that and don't bother him so much. I tell ya, Frank, we shouldn't be sitting here adding to his troubles."

Frank's face reddened. "Be quiet, Mario. Read your magazine."

Mario returned to his magazine. He riffled the pages of it, quietly at first and then with fury. Now his thin, green shirt was stained under the arms with sweat and there was sweat on his forehead. He pushed the magazine back and forth across his knees. "It's *my* epilepsy. I don't have to have it treated if I don't want. This doctor won't know how anyway. You know what he'll do? He'll ask me what seems to be the trouble. I'll tell him I got epilepsy. He'll feel my head. He might even X-ray it. Then he'll say, 'You got epilepsy. Where's your mother?' I'll say she's asleep. He'll say, 'Go wake her up and tell her I said you got epilepsy and should go to the country and live and take medicine every day and eat good.'"

Hugh said, "Mario—"

Mario turned on him. "You shut up. You don't know anything about this. I'm the one. I'm the one's been through this eight hundred thousand times. Not you. Or that nurse over there or the busy doctor. So shut up."

The nurse had come out from behind her desk and was walking across the room toward them. Her professional smile was fixed. She wove her way past the other patients and stood in front of them. She said, "Please try to be a little more quiet. You're disturbing the others here. I'm sure it won't be too much longer. Just please sit quietly."

"Faugh," said Mario and stood up. "Faugh to it all and

faugh to you! Tell the busy doctor I said that. Just faugh!"

There was nothing for Frank and Hugh to do but get up and follow Mario out. The three walked back down the avenue, pausing now and then to idly look at things in store windows. Frank was angry. Mario was pleased with himself. He pranced and capered. He darted into a store and came back out with six bananas. They passed a movie theater and he wiggled the bananas at the girl in the box office and whistled at her and made funny faces at her until she laughed. Frank and Hugh each accepted two of the bananas and they walked on down the street eating the fruit. Frank's disappointment and anger showed in the way he held himself aloof from Mario's antics. Mario was saying that it wasn't anything to have epilepsy and Frank was holding his anger.

"It ain't nothing," grinned Mario. "Just little ol' fits. They don't hurt. I don't even remember when I have them."

"Someday you'll die from one," muttered Frank. "You'll swallow your tongue or break your back and who's going to come to your funeral?"

"I'll make a good-looking corpse," grinned Mario. "Don't wake my mother up for my funeral. Just take her a rose from my coffin and let her smell it."

Frank threw his banana peels in the gutter and suddenly he was mad clean through. He whirled on Mario and grabbed him by both arms and shook him. "You don't know what you're saying! It could happen! Faugh to your mother and letting her smell a rose! You think that's funny? It ain't funny! You ain't funny when you're having one of your fits! You ain't good-looking! You look like death and destruction! You say faugh to that doctor back there? I say faugh to you! Faugh! Faugh! Faugh!"

Forever Hugh was to remember what happened to Mario

then; how his face began slowly to blanch, the whiteness appearing first around his mouth and then spreading, draining his cheeks and his earlobes, creeping up even into the roots of his hair. Mario began to chew his lips and smack them. Pulled by some invisible force his lips slowly began to be pulled back from his teeth. He began to gnash his teeth. There came his loud, sharp cry. He took two steps sideways and two backwards.

Frank had hold of him and was screaming to Hugh to help. "He's going to have one of his fits! He's going to fall! Hold him! Don't let him fall! Help me lay him down!"

There were people all around them and some of these were stopping to peer, some in neutral curiosity and some in odd reproach and some in horror. Now Mario was crazed. His face had gone from white to deepest purple and he was flailing, fighting, clawing, trying with a desperate strength to free himself. He was jerking up and down and back and forth and the saliva foaming from his mouth contained flecks of blood. His eyes had rolled back in their sockets and he didn't see and the people all around had drawn back to safer distances. With their hands over their mouths they were silently watching.

Gasping and being jerked and wobbled, Hugh and Frank had Mario between them and were trying to force him to an area of comparative safety—the doorway of a Christian Science Reading Room—but Mario broke away from them and staggered toward the curb and fell. The back of his head hit the concrete and he screamed once and was still.

Breathing hard, Hugh and Frank went to their friend and knelt beside him. Frank put his hand against Mario's cheek. "Mario? Mario?"

Mario wasn't breathing. He was dead.

88

Hugh heard the people who had watched all of this come to this realization. "He's dead," they said. "He was having a fit or something and those other two boys there were trying to help him. He hit his head on the curb. He's dead."

Crouched on the curb beside his dead friend, Frank was crying. His long black hair had fallen down across his face and he was saying, "So you're dead, Mario. So you're dead."

꧁ꘓ꧂

CHAPTER EIGHT

꧁ꘓ꧂

There came to the alley where the Proffitts lived a woman
with government credentials who sought the Proffitts' apartment and with veteran, impersonal zeal surveyed the painted
rooms and the plight of the family from Goose Elk. She strode
through the rooms once and did not look in any of the cupboards or closets. Her swift, skilled judgments lifted the Proffitts to a zone of breathable security. She said that shortly
they would start receiving money. She said that Dorman
Proffitt's blindness entitled them to yet further aid. Soon, she
said, another person from another agency would come and
talk with him.

She sat on a chair at Dorman Proffitt's side and at one
point during her conference with him drew the information
that Marvella was working for Mr. Zabowski. She was horri-
fied. "Only fourteen years old and working in a pawnshop?"
she cried. "Disgraceful! There are laws to protect our children, Mr. Proffitt. I'm afraid you haven't been very attentive
to them."

Shamefacedly Dorman Proffitt said, "I reckon you're right. I'll see to it she quits. I reckon I knowed all along it wasn't right for her to work there. Zollie and Juanita—I told you about them—they got her the job and then after they left we didn't know what else to do. A man came by here one day selling chinchillas; I bought a pair hoping to raise some more and sell 'em. I paid him ahead of time but he never delivered them. I think he was a crook of some kind'r another."

The government lady was looking at Dorman Proffitt. After a moment she said, "Your daughter must not go back to that pawnshop, Mr. Proffitt. She must sever her association with this Mr. Zabowski immediately. If she doesn't there might be consequences."

"Consequences," echoed Dorman Proffitt. "No, we wouldn't want none o' those. I'll see to it she quits. Don't worry, I'll see to it she quits today."

The free money was going to start coming. Their troubles were over.

"She was nice," said Hugh. "She didn't snoop. I'll have to remember to tell Frank. As soon as he gets over feeling so bad about Mario I'll tell him."

Though it was nearing suppertime Marvella went back to Zabowski's store to tell him she could no longer work for him. He opened the door to her and solemnly received the news. "That's all right," he said, and paid her for the entire week though there were two days lacking.

The Proffitts' supper that night was more substantial than had been planned. There was fried meat and potatoes and a store-bought cake with a ring of candied cherries on its top. This splurge finished consuming all but six dollars of Hugh's Loop money but that didn't matter. The free money was on its way. Pa had answered all the necessary questions and signed all the necessary papers.

Marvella washed and dried the supper dishes. The little kids, clustered around the television box in the front room, were being quiet. In his chair Pa dozed. An air of contentment and well-being pervaded.

Marvella hung her dish towel to dry and went to the window and looked down into the alley. By some accident of light or vision, Pa's trees, down at the far end of it, loomed actual in this moment. Standing in a wet mountain glen, surrounded by the wild, brilliant flora of the North Carolina mountains, the mimosa tree appeared distinct and immense. Marvella knelt at the window and looked at its wavering image for a long time. In a mood of delicious speculation she thought about her future self. She would become somebody important, like the government lady. This was possible now.

The check from the Government did not come as the government lady had promised. They waited three days and then four and still it did not come.

"Maybe," suggested Hugh, "they forgot where to send it. Or maybe somebody's stole it from our mailbox."

"Nobody could've done that," reasoned Dwain. "We meet the mailman every morning. What I think's happened is that they've forgot."

"Prob'ly," said Noah, "it will take months like Frank said. We should've asked her if it did. I didn't ask her. Did anybody else?"

The little kids looked at Marvella and at each other and shook their heads.

"We didn't think to ask—"

"Neither did Pa—"

"He didn't even think to ask her name. He said she told it to him once but he didn't think to ask her again. Now he can't remember it—"

"But she said soon—"

"She did not. She said shortly—"

"Well, that means the same thing."

Marvella paid the rent man with the last of Hugh's Loop money and spent the money she had earned at Zabowski's for food. In growing apprehension the Proffitts waited for the government check to come but it did not.

Marvella went to Zabowski's store to use his telephone. Mr. Zabowski had a new assistant, a serious young man with red cheeks and spectacles. Aloof to this particular piece of business but interested, he watched her dial the number she had dialed before and listened to her bewildered struggle with voices sharp and certain and voices soft and apologetic and voices pretentious and some not so pretentious but as perplexed as her own. Without a name, the lady who had promised the money could not be located. There were so many offices and so many cases. The Proffitts themselves were a case, one of thousands upon thousands. Status no doubt had been established. It was just that they couldn't find the lady who had visited the Proffitts and they couldn't find the file, if one had been made, concerning the Proffitts. There had been an office epidemic of colds and flu. The sick ones would be back in a few days. Then, no doubt, the Proffitts' file would be located and then, no doubt, the first check would be mailed.

Mr. Zabowski's new assistant was thoughtfully sipping hot tea from a glass. Marvella thanked him for the use of the telephone and went home and told Hugh that now they were a "case" but that the money this involved wasn't to be looked for any time soon.

"I knew it!" cried Hugh. "I knew it all the time! Everybody in this town's a liar! Nobody cares! Look at the way they did Mario! Even when he was *dead* he couldn't get anybody to pay attention to him! They let him lay on the street half an hour before they came and got him!"

"Hugh—"

Hugh put his hands through his hair. His eyes passionately challenged her. "Well, what we going to do? Just sit here and starve to death? I knew it all the time. Frank said it took months and I believe him now. But what we going to do? We can't wait months; we can't wait even another day. But is it a secret? Why are we down here in the alley talking about it? The others'll have to know. Won't they? Won't Pa and the little kids have to know?"

Marvella sat down on one of the lower steps leading up to their apartment. Assailed by an overmastering sense of homelessness, she sat with her head slightly bowed and the fear in her was a living thing. Out of the corner of her eye she could see the overflowing garbage cans and the stained mattress and the barren alley stretching away to the street. Nothing pretty or good had ever abided in this place. It was Godless. The people were Godless. Always so surly and mean. There was a particular meanness in this place and its people and there wasn't any way to best it except to be mean yourself.

The oily, yellow clouds massed in the sky over the alley weren't moving. Hugh was looking at her, waiting for her to speak. After a while she said, "Hugh, we won't tell Pa or the little kids. Go get Frank; tell him I want to see him."

"What for? He can't help us. He can't help hisself. He don't want to talk to nobody, Marvella. He feels bad about Mario. Very bad. He don't want to talk to nobody."

Marvella lifted her head and looked straight at her brother. "Go find him. Tell him I need to talk to him."

It was very late—close to midnight—and Marvella and Hugh and Frank were gathered around the Proffitts' table in their kitchen counting the night's take and comparing their experience of the night.

"Was you scared?" Frank asked Marvella.

She nodded. "Terrible. I thought I wouldn't be able to do it. I saw her—this woman—coming and I knew she was the one but I was scared so bad I wanted to run the other way. I looked at her shoes and they were nice—she had on a gold bracelet. I was scareder than I've ever been before in my whole life."

Hugh was putting his money and Marvella's together, taking his time to do this, yearning over the bills and silver as if he loved them. "But you did it," he said. "And now lookit all we've got. It's enough to buy us anything we want."

"No," said Marvella. "There's not that much here, Hugh. We'll still have to be careful. There's just enough here to tide us over till the government money comes."

"Faugh to the government money," said Frank. Since Mario's funeral he looked different. He had had his hair cut short, wore new black trousers, new shoes and socks, a new white shirt. His nails had been filed and cleaned. "Faugh to the Government," he said. "Who needs 'em? We could live like this forever. You see how easy it is. All you need is a little nerve and after a while that comes natural. After a while you don't even think about it any more."

Marvella put her hand out and touched the money that now

belonged to the Proffitts. "I don't think it would ever come natural to me. I was scared. Not of just the woman. It was . . . well. I don't want to talk about it any more."

"After a while," repeated Frank, "you don't even think about it. You just do it and come home and eat. It's just like a job except you don't have anybody standing around yelling at you all the time and you don't have to get up in the morning if you don't want. You got anything to eat?"

Marvella offered cocoa-water and Frank, with a shudder of distaste, said, "That's not even fit to drink. Where's your food? Haven't you got any food? Nev' mind. I see you don't. Wait a minute; I'll be right back." He went bouncing out of the apartment to his own place across the alley and presently came skipping back with an armload.

Outside the windows the strengthening starlight was washing the alley in pale, white light and the rats come scurrying from the buildings to forage among the garbage cans. Presently Frank went home to sleep and Marvella and Hugh went to their own beds.

Toward dawn Marvella's brain wonderfully came to a curiously peaceful compromise. Things beyond her power and perhaps even slightly beyond her comprehension had brought her and her family to this place—to this point—and now, except for their own resources they were abandoned. If there was any help for this they would have to find it themselves and do it themselves. Nobody can live just on a promise. Until the Government's promise was fulfilled and they could see it fulfilled they shouldn't believe in it. It didn't do anything for them. There was a difference in the people here; they didn't keep their promises. So different than back in Goose Elk. Back home when people said shortly they meant shortly, not days and days. And they didn't run off and hide after they'd made a promise. They kept their promises even if they were bad. The Critchers had promised to run the Proffitts out of the holler and they had. When you made a promise you kept it; it was the only way to do things. And you lived by the Golden Rule as much as you could. This wasn't always possible. Sometimes things got in between you and it. It was fine if everything else was at least tolerably equal. But when you had little brothers and a blind father at home hungry and there wasn't even rent money coming because your job was against the law, well, then you had to forget about doing to others as you would have them do unto you.

In the five o'clock dawn Marvella turned in her bed and before her brain came to a standstill she thought again of the woman in the good shoes and the gold bracelet. She was scared of me, thought Marvella. I was scared of me, too. I never thought I could do such a thing. I've changed. I did what I did tonight because there wasn't any other way but I'll never do it again. Tomorrow I'm going to get a job. *Somebody's* going to give me a job.

‹✢›

CHAPTER NINE

‹✢›

It was Frank's notion that the Proffitts' car could be restored to a useful life. One morning he and Hugh discussed this possibility. "We could put new tires on it," said Frank. "And fix up whatever's wrong under the hood and paint it."

Hugh squatted beside one of the front wheels. "It was sure pretty when we first got it. Pa was sure proud of it. But look at it now."

Frank had raised the hood of the car and was inspecting the complication of lines and wires beneath it. "I know a wino could tell us how to get it back to where it'd run again."

"What's a wino?"

Frank had his knife out and was tinkering with some of the wires. "A wino's a guy who drinks wine all the time. He gets rum-dum from it. Ain't you ever seen a wino?"

"No."

"There's one sleeps in here sometimes. Over there in the door. If we could find him he might be able to tell us how to fix this car. He might be sick though. He's sick a lot."

Hugh looked up at his friend. "What's he sick from?"

Frank bent to the wires, concentrating on the mysteries of their origins and functions. "From wine. All winos stay sick. My old man was a wino. I used to watch him. He'd get up in the mornings and drink a quart of wine and then he'd be sick. Then he'd lay down and go to sleep. Then he'd get up and drink another quart of wine. Then he'd be sick again. It used to make *me* sick watching him. I sure didn't shed any tears when he left. I was glad."

Hugh had risen to peer under the hood of the car also. Sometimes he didn't know how to take Frank. Frank said the funniest things about his parents. He sneered at his mother right to her face. When he gave her money he threw it at her. Almost every day he said how much he hated her.

Watching Frank poke at the wires, Hugh said, "Well, we might be able to get this thing running again. If you can get the wino to show us how. But what for? Marvella's the only one who could drive it and she's afraid to."

"Oh," said Frank, "she might not be afraid to always. Someday she might change her mind about being scared of it. Someday we might decide to take a little trip in it. We'll go look for the wino pretty soon. If he ain't sick or in jail he's out there somewhere wandering around."

"We'll eat first," said Hugh. "Before Marvella went off to look for another job this morning she fried us a whole chicken."

The little kids were lolling on the mattress. Each held a double strawberry ice cream cone and they were licking these and being absorbed in their own conversations. They were brown from their daily sun baths and they had taken on weight. All of the Proffitts had gained back the weight they had lost during the lean time they had waited for the government check to come. No more of that now though; no more waiting. Faugh to the Government and their money. The Proffitts could live without it.

Frank was saying, "It'll have to have new tires."

"They cost an awful lot," warned Hugh. "You going to pay for 'em?"

Frank turned his head sideways and grinned at Hugh. "Hillbilly."

"Well, are you?"

Gently Frank explained. "Hillbilly, you don't *buy* tires for a car. You steal 'em."

"Oh."

Frank let the hood of the car down. "But we got to find the wino first."

In the middle of the afternoon they found him sitting on a curb in the sun. Frank and Hugh sat down on opposite sides of him and the wino folded his day-old newspaper and gave his bleary attention.

"Wino," said Frank. "We've got a job for youse."

The wino jerked and drew back. "No."

"Now it ain't anything to get excited about," soothed Frank. "I shouldn't have said job. I should have said opportunity. I should have said we got an opportunity for youse."

Warily the wino relaxed. His watered, sorrowed eyes regarded Frank. After a moment he said, "I'm sick."

Frank nodded. "Sure you are. But we still got this opportunity for youse. We got a car we want you to help us fix up."

The wino shuffled his feet. He leaned and became vastly interested in them, decrepit in their shoddy shoes. He locked his hands around his knees and rocked back and forth, softly crooning to himself.

"It'll be worth two dollars to us," said Frank.

The wino continued to foolishly croon.

"Three then," said Frank. "And you can sleep on the mattress in our alley tonight. Hugh and me'll move it over up against the wall so's nobody will bother you."

The wino lost interest in his feet. He stilled them and his senseless song trailed away. He peered at Frank. "When would you pay me?"

"As soon's the job's done," replied Frank.

The wino's expression reflected a faint dignity. "No. I'll take half now and half when I finish."

Frank reached in his pocket and withdrew a one-dollar bill and a fifty-cent piece and handed the money to the wino. The wino got to his feet, went across the street and entered a store that had bottles in its windows.

"Old bum," said Frank.

For Marvella the day was one of frustration and failure. In search of a job and upon the advice of Frank she bought a newspaper and chose six possibilities. Then she took a bus to the Loop and made application to five stores and one movie theater. Nobody wanted to hire her. She was too young. She had no experience. She wasn't trained to do anything.

Someone said to her, "Go to an employment agency, why don't you?"

She looked hard at the speaker. "Could they find me a job?"

"They might," came the answer. "That's their business."

She found an employment agency and there filled out a card, giving her name, age, address, physical description, the place of her birth, the names of her living relatives. She had been required to state that she was not a high school graduate and that she did not possess any special skills. She had been obliged to part with several of her precious dollars for a registration fee. After that she was escorted to an airless cubicle for an interview. The interviewer was a bright young man with a theatrical smile and a bow tie. He spoke to her in the slightly lofty manner of a well-intentioned teacher: "Marvella Proffitt. That's a pretty name."

She twisted her feet around the legs of her chair. "Yes, sir."

The interviewer opened one of the drawers to his desk and withdrew a packet of small cards. Expertly he began to flick through them. In a minute he had finished scanning the whole stack. He frowned at the cards and smiled at Marvella. "It's hard when an applicant doesn't know how to do *anything*."

Marvella watched his hands shuffling the cards. He made a square pile of them and began sorting back through them. Soon his smile faded and he turned resentful. "There just isn't anything here," he complained. "I don't know why you people do it. Why do you come to the city when you don't know how to do anything? The competition is terrific. There are thousands of people like you walking around looking for jobs. Don't you know that?"

"I only know I need a job," answered Marvella. "I've *got* to have one. I've got four little brothers to look out for and my father. My father's blind. I've *got* to have a job."

The man looked away from her. His face had reddened. He picked up the packet of cards again and began sorting through them. "If you could type I could place you in a minute. And you're so *young*, dear."

"I could say I was older," said Marvella. "I only told you the truth because I thought I should. But I look older than I am. I could say I was eighteen or whatever they wanted. Would that hurt anything?"

The interviewer had come to a card that had caught his attention. He pulled it from the pack, read what was written on it and looked across at her. "Are you religious, dear?"

Doubtfully Marvella met his questioning gaze. Which would work best for her? To be religious or not religious? One had to be so careful with these people. Should she say she spent all of her Sundays on her knees in church or should she say she was a heathen? Maybe that's what this job called for, a heathen. No. Nobody expected you to be a heathen, not even these Chicago people. She formulated a prudent answer. "In a way I'm religious and in a way I'm not. I live mostly by the Golden Rule. Of course I don't know everything about life yet that maybe I should know. I've been thinking I might join a big church. Become a Catholic or something like that. I like revivals. Back home, when they have them, we always go. We like the singing. Everybody said I have a good singing voice. I like to sing hymns."

The interviewer was looking at her intently. "Do you know the Bible?"

"The Bible? Oh, sure. I know all about it. I'm a Christian. One time when I was in first grade I won a prize for knowing all the books of the Bible by heart. Genesis, Exodus, Leviticus, Deuteronomy, First and Second Kings, First and Second Chronicles, Ruth—"

"Do you think you could be an assistant to a lady minister?"

"A lady minister? I didn't know they had lady . . . well, sure. Sure I could."

The interviewer was writing an address on a card. He looked at her again only once to say that if she got the job she should come back and see him about the fee which would be half of one month's salary.

She left the employment agency and went out on the street again. She stood on a corner studying the card that had been given to her. She had a job. Well, the promise of one anyway. She smiled at a person who didn't smile back and pursed her lips and whistled. She saw her bus coming and ran to catch it.

Only to Hugh could Marvella relate the account of her experience with the lady minister: "It was in an old rickety building that we wouldn't even have let a dog sleep in back in Goose Elk. Everybody else on the street it was on had moved out. There was just her in this awful old building that was falling down. The windows were all painted black. You should have seen it. You should have seen her, too. She had a big, wooden cross around her neck. I swear it must've weighed ten pounds. And sandals and a long, white dress. She was crazy; I know she was. There was something wrong with her. I went in and told her my name and gave her the card from the employment agency and she told me to sit down but then she forgot I was there. She just kept walking around laughing and singing and talking to herself and every once in a while she'd run over to a big bell that was hanging from the ceiling and ring it. She didn't pay a bit more mind to me than if I hadn't even been there so after a while I just got up and left. I went back to the employment agency and told that man about it and asked him to give me my money back but he wouldn't. He said they didn't make refunds."

Hugh wasn't terribly interested. He was making himself a

thick meat sandwich. "Forget it," he said. "Just forget it. Faugh to it. We'll get along."

Marvella watched Hugh dribble catsup, completing the sandwich. She sat down in a chair opposite him, resting her elbows on her knees. "No," she said. "No, we've got to have jobs. We've got to be decent. That other was an emergency but it shouldn't happen again. We can't let it. We've got to have jobs and work for our living and be decent."

Hugh lifted his overweight sandwich and took a bite of it and chewed. "Good," he commented. "I like cold roast meat. Don't look so worried, Marvella. It'll be all right. Everything's going to be all right."

Marvella hitched her chair toward the window and looked down into the alley. There was going to be a new tenant in the building across the way. He had just arrived in a taxi and the driver was helping him unload his bags and boxes. Frank was there, too, capering around and offering bits of offhand advice. He was talking very loud. What he was saying was clearly audible to Marvella: "You shouldn't let the driver just dump you out here, mister. It's a long climb up them stairs and them boxes look heavy. Hey, mister, I hope you brought yourself a fan. If you didn't you better go out and buy yourself one. It's so hot sleeping up there even the roaches leave at night."

The driver of the taxi was ignoring Frank. He set the last bag out, straightened and turned to the new tenant to receive his pay. The money exchanged hands, the taxi drove off, and the new tenant looked up toward the windows where Marvella watched. There was the distance between them, gray and wavering-dim, the way air is at the beginning of nightfall, but still it seemed to Marvella that the eyes of this stranger met hers and connected with hers in some secret way. The stranger smiled and she smiled back. She watched him lift a bag and a box and carry them the few steps to the entrance to the building. After a minute Frank picked up one of the bags and followed.

This man who had come to live in the building across the alley from the pink apartment became important to the Proffits. He was in a little business for himself—a messenger business he called it—and he offered Hugh and Marvella jobs. He gave them parcels to deliver to persons living in other parts of the city and for these deliveries he paid five dollars each plus carfare. His name was Cedric Bannister and he was neither very young nor very old but a pleasant in-between age. He urged them to call him by his first name and was very friendly. He was generous, too. Sometimes he wanted packages delivered at night and for these he always paid a dollar or two more.

Cedric offered Frank a job but Frank declined it. "There's something funny about that guy," he said. "If he's in the messenger business why don't he have a phone? And why don't he have a truck or at least a car? And why does he have to hire youse guys to do his delivering for him? What's in them packages you deliver for him anyway? You ever look?"

Hugh and Marvella shook their heads. "No."

"Hillbillies," said Frank. "Listen, hillbillies, you shouldn't trust everybody the way you do. Sure Cedric looks nice and he talks nice but that don't mean anything. Maybe he's a big crook, mixed up in something he shouldn't ought to be. And you're getting mixed up in it, too."

"We aren't mixed up in anything," said Marvella. "We're just working for Cedric. I admit it's not like any other job

106

we've ever had but it's a good job and it'll do until something better comes along."

Frank laughed and trotted off and Hugh and Marvella finished washing down the stairway which didn't need to be washed because it had just been done the day prior. The Proffitts did not know what to do with their time; there was too much of it. So they slept more than they were accustomed to sleeping, spent hours on the preparation of meals, washed things that didn't need washing, and watched television. When Cedric wanted packages delivered Hugh or Marvella would deliver them. Sometimes this would only take a few minutes and sometimes it would take hours. Hugh and Marvella did not talk to Cedric's customers because Cedric had told them not to. They just delivered the packages, all shapes and sizes of them, and came back home.

Cedric was a college graduate and could speak on almost any subject with authority. His father owned a shoe factory in New England, was very wealthy, and had had high ambitions for Cedric to become somebody important—a diplomat to a foreign country or a bank president—but Cedric said he preferred his own kind of life. He liked living in his two rooms in the alley. Out of his boxes he furnished the rooms nice and kept them neat and lived quietly.

All of the Proffitts liked Cedric. They thought he was a good man and they wouldn't let Frank even hint that he might be otherwise.

But one afternoon the police came and arrested Cedric. It was a quiet proceeding; the police came into the alley and parked their car in front of the doorway to Cedric's building, went up the stairs and presently came back down leading Cedric. They had his boxes and his bags and they put these and Cedric in the back seat of the car and drove off. Cedric didn't even look in the direction of the Proffitts' building nor did he look back as he was borne away.

Frank was triumphant. He said, "See, I told you he was a big crook of some kind. I told you he was a phony baloney. Those clunkheads wouldn't tell me what they were arresting him for but I think I know. I think Cedric was peddling drugs."

The Proffitts looked at each other and Frank. "Drugs?"

Frank returned their looks and after a long moment he said, "I'm not talking about the kind of drugs you buy in a drugstore. There's another kind that you buy from guys like Cedric. Well, don't you know about drugs?"

"No," replied the Proffitts.

They didn't know what Frank was talking about. They only knew that they had lost a friend and their jobs. They went out and looked for others but did not find them.

CHAPTER TEN

The summer was almost accomplished. Now the days were slowly shortening and the nights slowly lengthening. Each morning the sun came sliding into the alley just a little later, still bright and hot, but with little rifts of autumnal coolness behind it. As the day deepened the coolness dissipated but late in the afternoon it came back. Soon there would be a seasonal change.

How the Proffitts had managed to survive the summer frightened Marvella whenever she allowed herself to think of it so she didn't permit herself to dwell on it often. From time to time she and Hugh would talk casually about going back to Goose Elk where living was cheaper and somehow simpler. They'd get out the road maps that Zollie had left in the glove compartment of the car and study the route they'd have to take and talk about how much it would cost. Once in a real mood of dissatisfaction and longing they bought a city map and charted a course that would take them out of the alley and the city and out on the highway leading back to North Carolina. But then they faced the reality of what was there; their enemies, the Critchers, the diseased fields, the hard winter that lay ahead. In Goose Elk all you could do with the winter was wait it out and if you didn't have a store of food laid by you'd starve while you were waiting. Studying the maps and considering the impossible flight, Hugh and Marvella looked at each other and were dismayed and convinced.

"We'd never make it through the winter," said Hugh. "We'd starve to death 'fore Christmas."

Marvella shivered.

Hugh gnawed at his nails. "I wonder what other people do who're in the same fix we're in. There must be some. We can't be the only ones. What do you reckon they do?"

"I don't know," replied Marvella. "I'm not thinking about other people. I'm thinking about us. I'm going to get a job. Somebody in this town is going to give me a job."

"Yeh," said Hugh in deepest disgust and still gnawing his nails left the apartment and went down to the alley to meet Frank.

Marvella mopped the kitchen that didn't need to be mopped and listened to the wrangling of the little kids; they were bickering over which television program they would watch. Most days she could tolerate their whining and shouting but today her nerves were raw. Viciously she slammed her tin mop bucket against the stove and the soapy water in it sloshed out and she ran into the front room and yelled at the little kids to either shut up or get themselves murdered and they jumped up and ran out.

In his chair in the corner Dorman Proffitt was dozing. He opened his eyes and turned his head in her direction. "What's the matter?"

"Nothing," she answered and went back to her kitchen mopping.

Marvella had toughened. Now the little kids jumped when she spoke. Sometimes she had to secretly laugh at the way they jumped to obey her but more often than not it wasn't funny. Nothing was.

Marvella had discovered indifference. One day a woman who said she was from the Government came to call on the Proffitts, to inquire if their needs were being sufficiently cared for and Marvella had had herself a fine time.

"Any problems?" asked the woman.

Marvella shrugged. "Sure. We've got plenty of problems. Our main one is to stay alive. But I didn't think anybody was interested."

Standing on the landing just outside the Proffitts' door, the woman shifted her purse and the brown leather case she carried. She was young and very pretty but there was something wrong with her eyes. She kept blinking them. "I thought I might have a little talk with your father," she said.

"Yes'm," said Marvella. "But he's asleep."

The woman glanced at her watch. "Couldn't you wake him? I don't have much time. I should talk with him."

"About what, ma'am? My father doesn't know anything about the Government. He's blind. I'm the one who takes care of everything. We've got nothing to do with the Government. We don't owe them anything. They aren't doing anything for us."

The woman had taken some papers from her case. Frowning, she scrutinized them. "Aren't you receiving any aid from us?"

Marvella leaned against the door casing and played with the ends of her long, red hair. "No'm. Some time back I phoned some government office—I forgot the name of it now. Anyway, they sent a woman out and she said we'd start getting some money shortly but it's never come. I quit my job, too, just on her say-so and couldn't get it back. It was against the law, she said. Isn't that funny? I tried some other places but nobody'd hire me. I'm too young, they said. Law me, back where we come from nobody's too young to work but they do things different here. We found that out. Anyway we're making out the best way we can. If you people ever get around to sending us a check we'll appreciate it. But if you can't, don't worry about it. We've been getting enough money from other people to keep us going."

It had been an embarrassing thing for the representative from the Government. She had apologized all the way down the steps and out to her car. Fervently she had promised to see to it that the Proffitts got some aid. "Immediately," she said. "I'll see to it immediately."

It wasn't a good promise. Days went by and more days and the aid didn't come.

The Proffitts continued to live.

It was a Saturday night and Marvella was tired and dejected. Her own sortie to the Loop had been near fruitless: two one-dollar bills and a strand of junky, glass beads. The woman had been well dressed, too, had stepped from her cab like she was somebody rich. She was a fraud, that's what she was; all that expensive-looking fur slung around her neck and those fancy gloves. Coming out of that taxi so snooty and bigety—pretending to somebody—herself maybe—that she was on her way to someplace important, but then just sauntering down the avenue alone. People sure were phony.

The darkness was thick at the windows and Marvella sat,

waiting for Hugh and Frank to come. She heard their footsteps running in the alley and then on the stairway and rose and went quickly to the door to unbolt it. The two boys pushed past her and went directly to the kitchen and began emptying the contents of their pockets on the table. They were very excited.

"Is everybody asleep?" asked Hugh. "Something happened. Wait'll you hear. Look, I tore my pants."

Frank had sat down and was trying to catch his breath. He stood up and went to the door separating the kitchen from the front room and closed it. He shoved his hands through his hair and started walking up and down. "Faugh to your torn pants," he said to Hugh. "They ain't anything. We might've been killed. What'd you yell for?"

Hugh had trouble assembling his speech. "I was trying . . . well, you pushed her! I saw you! It wasn't you who was almost killed! It was her and me! That's what I yelled for! That's what for! And . . . you just kept pushing . . . your own mother! Whatsa matter with you? You crazy?"

"What—" said Marvella. "What—"

Hugh was shivering. His face was white and he was gnawing at his nails with his teeth. Shrilly he began to explain. "We was just standing there waiting for the bus . . . we was all through with our work and we was just standing there waiting for the bus when she . . . Frank's mother . . . came up and said could he give her some money. Well, then . . . Frank said he could . . . only he didn't . . . the bus came . . . and he pushed her and I tried . . . I tried to grab her back . . . I grabbed her back . . . but Frank, he pushed us both. . . ."

"It was an accident," stated Frank and his voice was very gentle and his black eyes were softly ashine. "You're getting it all mixed up. I bumped into her because somebody was pushing me and then you got in the way and I pulled you back. If I hadn't, you'd have been killed. What'd you yell for? You weren't hurt."

Hugh was fiercely gesticulating. "She fell down . . . in front of the bus . . . and it hit her and then everybody got off . . . the driver, he said . . . he said he didn't see her . . . and then somebody . . . somebody went for the police . . . and then Frank made me . . . he said we shouldn't get mixed up in it . . . and then . . . then we ran away. Before the police came."

Frank had risen; he had gone to the window to look out across the alley. Marvella looked at his back and then at Hugh. He was staring at her. For an unconscionable time there was only the silence in the room, filling it, and then Frank came back from the window and sat down again and began to count the money. "She ain't dead," he said. "I saw her. All it did was bang her up a little. It was an accident. They'll take good care of her in the hospital."

The two Proffitts watched Frank counting the money and no one spoke again of what had happened.

Frank finished counting the money, careful to keep his take apart from Hugh's, and then with only a nonchalant, "See youse tomorrow," left the pink apartment, skipped down the stairs and across the alley. From their window Marvella and Hugh watched him disappear into the blackness of his own building.

"He did it," whispered Hugh. "I saw him. Maybe that part . . . him pushing me was an accident . . . I think it was . . . but he meant to . . . I saw him push her . . . it wasn't no accident."

Marvella breathed and breathed again. The sound of breath filled her ears like rushing wind. Sickeningly she felt her heart turn and through and through her she felt the sudden lunge of real terror. Astonishingly she recognized the cause of the fear. I'm afraid, she thought, of us. Of what's happened to us. What we've become; the way we've changed. How we can hear and see and do such terrible things and afterward go to sleep. Look at us now. We're standing here now shocked to our roots because of what happened tonight but in a little while we'll go to bed and go to sleep and tomorrow Frank will come and eat with us and right along with him we'll act like tonight just never happened. That's the way we are now. We've become like Frank. Worse. We've become worse than him. Because we know about other things and he doesn't. Now we aren't natural the way we were back in Goose Elk. I'm afraid of us. We've got to go back to where things and people are natural.

Marvella pressed her hand against her ribs and breathed and in this isolation her inherent values came out of the pit where they had been hiding and showed themselves to her and were acknowledged. She spoke. "Hugh."

"It wasn't no accident, Marvella. He did it. I saw him."

"Hugh."

"What?"

"I'm afraid. Of us. Of what's happened to us. Things have got away from us. We don't think right any more."

"Yes," whispered Hugh. "Yes."

"We've got to go back. To Goose Elk. Now. Tomorrow. Before something real bad happens."

"Yes," whispered Hugh. "But . . . but how?"

"We'll go in the car. I'll drive us."

"I thought you was afraid to drive."

"I am but I'll do it anyway."

"It'll take money. What will we do for money?"

"I have a little and then there's this—what you brought tonight."

Hugh turned from the window and looked at the money lying on the table. "I don't want us to use that money. I wish I could give it back."

"You can't, Hugh. There's no way. So we'll use it to get back to Goose Elk."

Hugh had his head in his hands. His face was whitely glistening. He dropped his hands. "Yes. All right. But, Marvella, Frank'll want to go with us. That's why he got the tires for the car. He didn't say so but I know it. He'll want to go with us."

"Frank can't go with us, Hugh."

"Can't?"

"No."

"Because—"

"Because he's not like us. We're different than he is and I . . . I just don't want him around any more. We'll go tomorrow night. By ourselves. I think it'll be easier driving at night; there won't be as much traffic. So we'll go tomorrow night."

"Yes," whispered Hugh. "Yes."

They told their father of their decision the next morning and he rose from his chair and without anyone guiding him went to his room and began emptying the dresser drawers, laying his clothes in piles on the bed.

The little kids screamed their delight:

"We're going home!"

"Back to Goose Elk—"

"Wonder will the Critchers still be there—"

" 'Course they'll be—"

"Home—"

"No more playing in the alley—"

116

"We hate the alley—"

"It stinks—"

"The smoke makes me cough—"

"Faugh to this place. Faugh on it."

"Don't ever," said Marvella, "say that word again."

The little kids gazed at her with their eyes gone wide and quiet.

"If I ever hear you say it again I'll whip you," said Marvella. "It's a bad word. It isn't for us to use. You understand?"

The little kids nodded.

Hugh went after cardboard boxes to pack their things in and Marvella went down the stairs and across to the car. It would have to be backed to the stairs so that they could pack it. Tonight she would have to drive it out of the alley and out onto the streets. She'd have to drive it through the city and out of it. She'd have to do it all by herself. Pa wouldn't be any help and neither would Hugh. The little kids would probably make her nervous and the traffic, whizzing in all directions, was certain to. It'd sure be a lot different than driving a pickup out in an open field.

After a minute Marvella opened the door on the driver's side of the car and got in. I'm scared, she thought, and put the key in the ignition and turned it. She backed the car to the stairway and got out of it.

Frank was coming across the alley. With her foot on the lowest step Marvella turned and waited for him. Grinning, he capered up to her. "You going for a ride, Marvella? Where's Hugh and the other kids? Hey, I got an idea. Let's all go for a little ride. Ride out to the country and see what's there. Get a look at something different for a change. It'll do us all good, huh?"

Marvella removed her foot from the step and turned and faced him. "Frank, we're going back to North Carolina tonight."

Frank's grin faded. Something in his eyes shifted. He hooked his thumbs in his belt. When he spoke his voice vibrated with some hidden passion. "I'm going with you. I want to go with you."

"No, Frank."

Frank moved toward her and stopped. "Yes. I want to go with you. You've got to let me."

Marvella lifted her hands. "Frank, I can't let you."

"Why not?"

"Because."

"That's no reason. What's the reason?"

"I can't explain it. It's something . . . well, we aren't the same. You think different than we do. You . . . what you think is all right is not all right. Not with us. If you went with us you'd bring . . . I wouldn't be able to change you to our way of thinking. Your way of thinking and our way is too different. Besides there's your mother."

Frank sneered. "Faugh to my mother."

Marvella was silent. The desire to get things straight between them—to somehow help him—was a real want but she couldn't find the words.

Frank, with his sneer growing, was saying, "My way of thinking wasn't so different from yours before. It kept you from starving. There wasn't anything wrong with it when you was hungry. I was the one showed you the way and you were glad to find it but now, all of a sudden, I'm not good enough for you."

"Frank, that's not it—"

"Them are my tires you're going on and I had the wino fix up the car."

"I know you did. I'll pay you for the tires. I'll pay you whatever you want. How much do you want?"

With a flat, bitter look Frank was accepting defeat. "I stole 'em. The money you'd pay me with was stolen, too. I don't want you to pay me. I just want . . . I just wanted to . . ." Suddenly he was shouting. "Oh, faugh on you! I don't want anything from you, you dumb hillbilly! Go on back to where you came from! I hope you kill yourself on the way! I hope you all get killed! Hillbilly! Dumb! Faugh on you! Just faugh on you!" He whirled and ran back across the alley and disappeared into his own building.

Marvella was surprised to find herself trembling. She had to wait for the violent beating of her heart to quiet before she could climb the stairs. Somebody should help him, she thought. But it can't be me. I don't know how. I don't know enough. I would have to undo all that's been done to him and I just wouldn't know how.

That night the Proffitts left the pink apartment and the alley. While they were arranging themselves in the car they looked for the last time at the row of garbage cans and the stained mattress. Above the alley the sky was clear. Mrs. Haliki's apartment was dimly lighted. They could see her moving around in her kitchen. She lifted a steaming kettle from the stove and carried it to the sink. She bent and poured and the steam enveloped her head.

"She never even said hey to us," commented Noah. "All the time we lived here she didn't."

Arlie and Dwain were fighting over who would sit next

to the window. Dorman Proffitt, in the passenger side of the front seat, turned and spoke to them sharply. "You little kids be quiet now. This is going to be a little nerve-wracking for Marvella. Hush now. All of you. You can fight when we get home."

Marvella had started the car. She turned her head and looked at her father. Eons ago she had promised herself that he would go back to Goose Elk wearing a new hat and a fine, new suit with a twenty-dollar bill stuck in the breast pocket of it. Instead he was going back in the same old clothes he had come in. It seemed important that she clear the air of the lie concerning the trees. "Pa," she said. "There aren't any trees growing in here. Not a mimosa or any other kind. That was just a story I made up."

Her father clasped his hands around his knees. He lifted his chin. After a moment he said, "Well, I didn't see how they could. This air ain't fitting for anything to breathe. I'm glad to be going from here. We all set?"

"All set back here," called out Hugh. "Let's go."

The car moved down the alley and left it.

‹§›

CHAPTER ELEVEN

‹§›

They came into the hollow between the mountains and the town of Goose Elk, which lay just over the ridge, early in the morning of the third day of travel. They sat forward in their seats and looked and listened and smelled.

A white, glistening mist lay over the hollow. Every leaf and bush was decorated with it. From a high ridgetop, in a realm of sourwood trees turned shimmering red with the advancing autumn, there came the brilliant, vigorous song of a winter wren. The air was fine and clean.

Marvella turned the car into the narrow, rutted road that led up to the Proffitts' tar-papered house. During these last hours of the journey the little kids had been cranky but now they sat with eyes shining, staring out across the hollow to the spiral of gray smoke rising from the Critchers' house. They whispered among themselves.

Dorman Proffitt had sat up straighter in his seat and was smiling. They jounced over a particularly big rut and he said, "I remember that 'un. It's where your mama and me felled a big beech the day we started clearing this land. Reckon we didn't do such a good job of it. Just take yourselves a good, long whiff o' this air, kids. Eh law!"

The little kids could hardly wait for the car to stop. When it did they tumbled from it and ran around and around, rediscovering things and yelping:

"It's just like we left it!"

"Ain't anything changed!"

" 'Course not. What could change?"

"Look, Zollie's flowers are still growing."

"It's cold!"

"Well, naturally! We're in the mountains! We're home!"

"Let's get some wood and build a fire in the fireplace."

"There ain't any chopped."

"Well, chop some!"

Dorman Proffitt had stepped from the car and was going up the steps of the cabin alone. He had the key to the door in his hand and was unlocking it.

Marvella got out of the car and stretched her aching legs. She walked across the yard to the bed of flowers that Zollie had taken such pains to bring down from the mountains and replant. There were only a few late bloomers left: some beautifully bright orange blossoms of pleurisy root, some rose-colored Aaron's-rod, and a few stems of pilewort.

She walked around the bed twice and then stood still beside it. She thought of Zollie. Where was she now? Not dead. Whatever else, Zollie wasn't dead. Zollie would never die. There was too much life in her. She liked to fight too much. She fought like a man. She could heft a full-grown man without even breathing hard. The times she had done that to Mr. Critcher, running up to him from behind to grab him and lift him, laughing at the way his feet dangled and his embarrassment. Zollie had liked to humiliate people.

They were home. That much had been accomplished. Now if they died of starvation at least they'd do it in their own home, on their own land. Chicago had been a bad, bad mistake. It would take forever to forget it. Maybe they wouldn't ever. She wouldn't. That terrible place. The awful, worrisome time they'd had. Stealing. How could you ever forget that you had actually stolen? It was impossible to just lift pieces from your mind. To say the reason to yourself didn't help much. Anybody can think of a reason for a wrongdoing. The part that was so bad was that she'd never be able to pay. Or even say she was sorry.

The Critchers were coming across the hollow, the whole family of them, the little kids running on ahead of mister and missus, whooping like savages. Probably they're coming to fight some more, thought Marvella, and went down the slope to meet them. Each of them carried something wrapped in newspaper or gunnysacking and when they were within shouting distance they started yelling:

"Hey there, Proffitts! You-all home from Chicago?"

"We saw you coming and couldn't believe our eyes!"

"You're home for good, ain't you?"

"Where's Zollie?"

"Where's the little kids?"

"Where's your pa?"

They came up to her and clustered around her excitedly, pressing their gifts. "When we saw you coming we just grabbed whatever we could lay our hands on," shouted Mrs. Critcher. "Ain't none of it fancy but it'll keep you from going hungry till you can get settled. Where's Zollie? Did you say?"

Marvella looked at Mrs. Critcher and shook her head. In horror she felt tears starting. "Zollie left us right after we got to Chicago. Her and her sister ran off somewhere's together and . . . and the police couldn't find them and . . . and then the government people said they'd help us . . . but they didn't . . . and Hugh and I . . . Hugh and I . . ."

Mrs. Critcher was maneuvering herself so that she could stand between Marvella and the rest of the Critchers. She thrust the parcel she carried into the hands of Jody, who was Hugh's age. "What're you gawking at? Ain't you ever seen anybody glad to be home before?"

"She's bawling," said Jody with curious eyes.

Mrs. Critcher thumped Jody's head with her knuckles. "She ain't either. She's laughing. 'Cause she's so glad to be home. Go find Mr. Proffitt and tell him his neighbors is out here. No, wait a minute. We'll all go inside. You look like you're ready to keel over, Marvella. You had breakfast yet? You ain't? I'll cook you some. We brought eggs and ham and milk and, law, I don't know what all. When we saw you coming we just grabbed whatever we could lay our hands on."

The Critcher kids were running toward the house and the Proffitt kids were coming out of the door to meet them. Between Hugh and Jody there was a moment of hesitation and then they flung their arms around each other.

Mr. Critcher was saying, "The blight hit us, too, Marvella. Right after you folks left. But I got the county people out here and now we know what caused it. I'll talk to your pa about it. I don't think it'll happen again. We won't let it."

And Mrs. Critcher was saying, "Everybody in town asked about you. They've been mad at us for running you off. But that's all over now; you're home now. People will help you get started again; everybody around here will. You'll see. Come on now, stop your blubbering. There ain't anything to blubber about. We know it was a bad time for you. It was a bad time for us, too. We liked to have died from loneliness but it's all over now."

Marvella was openly weeping. She couldn't stop. She was crying for the friendless man who had died on the stained mattress lying in the alley back in Chicago. For the old sick wino who slept in doorways and for Cedric, the drug peddler. She was crying for Mario and for Frank and for Mrs. Haliki. For Hugh and herself. For all that had been found and lost in Chicago.